The Rats of Grandville

By G. England Lowry

This is a work of fiction. Names, characters, places and incidents are the product of the author's imagination or are used fictitiously, and any resemblance to actual persons, living or dead, business establishments, events, or locales is entirely coincidental.

THE RATS OF GRANDVILLE
Copyright © 2012 by G. England Lowry

ISBN 978-0-615-73031

Printed in USA by 48HrBooks (www.48HrBooks.com)

ACKNOWLEDGMENTS

Normally, no one I know suddenly announces to the world, "I'm going to write a book" and starts in without first being inspired and then later helped along the way by some very caring people." "The Rats of Grandville" came to life only because of an incredible group of very talented women in Granbury, Texas who provided the initial inspiration; reaching out to me with their friendship, artistic talent, personalities, and support all along the way.

Thank you to The Makers: They know who they are, and this book is for them. I love them all, and they will remain in my heart forever.

Thank you to Julie Pitts and BB French who generously provide a gathering place and guidance for all fiber artisans to meet and create every day. Without their unselfish efforts, none of us would have the comfort of coming together in such a loving atmosphere.

Thank you to all of my patient editors along the pathway: including Patti Purvis who taught me to knit, and Pat Stevens who encouraged me to continue when I had doubts, Waynell Harris, my main editor, and my readers Laverne Briscoe, Connie Melton, Sheila Wilde, and also to Christi Dotter, who pushed me to print this, thank you, all.

Thank you to my family; especially my husband Bob, who continuously provides surprising ideas and solutions for the rats, never asking once, "What was I thinking?" never doubting my sanity, and with a sincere constant reminder, "Never give up!"

Thank you Bob, for never complaining about my yarn purchases, and asking where I have it all stashed...

I have been very blessed in my life to know all of these people. I have discovered that the opportunity for women to come together and work magic with their hands not only produces something beautiful to hold, but provides the unplanned surprise of lifelong friendships and memories that are cherished forever. Oh, what fun we have!

Even if you don't knit or crochet, or weave, spin, or hook; go to a yarn shop. Walk around, pick up some yarn; put it to your cheek: feel the fiber of the place! And take your time to look around. Join those at the gathering table who ask you to join them, because they will ask, you know. You'll be hooked for life (pardon the pun) and who knows? You may end up making a rat!

Happy reading. This book will make you smile.....

G. England Lowry

THE ORIGINAL RAT MAKERS GENEALOGY

We all have roots. It is important for many of us to recognize this. Many of us are very proud of our family history, making sure we broadcast "who our great-great grandfathers were and there are some of us we would like to keep those family skeletons in the closet. This is no different for The Rats of Grandville. Our heritage details we are all "begat" from someone, and so goes the rats only difference being they are:

"Be-rat"; not "begat"!

Therefore, please find the Rats Family Tree a little helpful with your reference. You can flip back to this page as you begin your journey with the Makers.

MAKER	"BE-RAT"	BORN
Judy Paxton	Chloe*	2009*
	Lenny	2010
	Sir Reginald**	2010
	Violet	2011
DD Bench	Ratcliff	2009
	Bella	2011
	Beauty***	***
	Bonnie***	***
Raspberry Simms	Rattina	2011
Geraldine	Pierre	2011
Marna	Antonius Le Beau	2011
Sandy	El Ratoncito Perez	2011
Katy Smith	Echo	2011
Mary Ellen Afton	Sheriff Tex	2011
Anita Stanley	Amelia Earrat	2011

* No one really knows when Chloe was born; she was there on the table before the Makers came

** A gift to Samantha, owner of the Art Gallery, who formally named him

*** In the "making" at the time of this book writing; still yet to be born

Chapter One

The Yarn Shop

Who would have thought? Magic arrives in many forms, but discovered alive and well and thriving in a simple little yarn store tucked away in a little Texas country town? And the magicians being a collection of unassuming grandmother-type looking ladies toting a bunch of knitting needles under their arms?

And here's the best part: they didn't even know they were magicians.

No One... not even a soul... would have thought.

So you may be surprised then, when all year long, tucked away in a quaint little art shop located in Grandville, Texas, population about 5000, in the late afternoons, about six or eight ladies take a journey together. Even in the coldest days, when the temperature is only twenty degrees, they come.

Bundled up tight in their own knitted hats, scarves and sweaters, they slowly parade their way up a rickety winding stairway to the loft above. It is challenging for them but worth their effort, for perched at the top and overlooking over the gallery below, there it is: The tiny Yarn Shop, cozy and warm and waiting for them. They come to knit, crochet, and weave magic with their needles. And they come to talk and laugh, and share their life stories.

Some days, they even come to vent about something, but most times, they simply come to relax and enjoy each others company, and make something beautiful. These hours in the loft are coveted. They wait all week long for this cherished time together. Nothing much keeps knitters away from their gathering.

The shop is owned by Judy Paxton, and her Partner, "DD" Bench, well known all over Texas for their knitting and famous teddy bear making skills, not to mention their instruction classes for beginners.

Inspiration peaks out from every corner, and, over the past several years, they have established a very profitable little fiber arts business. Judy and "DD" look very much alike, but they are not sisters. They could be twins: they are the same age, both have light blonde hair cut in a bob-style.

They are very current and keep up with all the latest fashion trends. Sometimes they talk and laugh at the same time and their customers love their animated conversations. They both "dress" for the day at the shop in fashionable garb accented with scarves and vests they have created themselves. "Fiber Fashionistas" who know marketing skills well.

DD always wears some kind of artsy teddy-bear necklace because bears are her trademark. Everyone in town knows these shop owners, that they teach people to knit and crochet, and make "memory bears" for keepsake gifts. Even though the space is small, this is the fourth location for The Yarn Shop, as they have grown from secondary locations to this main-street location where everyone can easily see it and park close by. Convenience is important when you are a Grandmother toting a purse and a heavy knit bag at the same time.

The shop window displays always have a "stop you in your tracks" knitted piece that grabs your attention and begs you to come on in and look a little closer. "I wonder if I could make that," you think, and bingo, another knitter is born.

You have to enter through The Art Gallery gift shop on the first level and walk to the back of the store where the spiral stairway is located, and then grab a wobbly hand rail, balance yourself, and work your way to the top. But the climb is well worth the trip because even if you are not a knitter, it's a fun place to investigate.

The Yarn Shop loft space is just one room with no bathroom or kitchen. It is a very tight area, and you can't help but bump into things making your way around. There are no walls, and you can look over the guard rail and see The Art Gallery and hear the customers below. It is very warm and cozy, with just enough room for a large antique Country French table situated in the middle. Judy and DD have provided six canvas director-style chairs that comfortably seat their fellow customer friends of all sizes.

Someone has climbed the stairs to get water for the coffeepot, as the smell of freshly brewed pecan flavored coffee waffles from somewhere behind a shelf. Friends gather here. One of them once said of the place, "Our table is like our secret childhood tree house. We come to build. To create, to escape, and share our most personal stories with those we love."

Sheer medicine for the heart and soul. Sometimes, the days get busy, and the group of knitters will expand beyond the six available chairs, so a newcomer will reach behind a curtain in the back of the shop that hides storage shelves and pull out an additional folding chair. There are always loud cheers of welcome and chatter and even clapping as yet another member has made it up the stairs joining the group, which can sometimes grow to twelve or more. The loft exudes happiness. All around the room, in every direction, and from floor to ceiling, there is yarn. It just oozes with yarn. Stacks of it and shelves of it, and baskets of yarn everywhere: Rainbows of fuzz, some with multi-colors and specks, some with glitzy gold and silver intertwined, and some that are "au-natural," meaning they are hand-spun with wool fiber from alpacas and llamas raised locally. These are very soft, and force you to take them immediately to your cheek for a "softness check". The colors and textures are dizzying. There is so much yarn its like living inside a sweater! If you are a knitter, and you live within fifty miles, you would know this place, and you would come here to buy your yarn, needles, looms, spinners, and all tools necessary for your craft. And you would come for ideas, support, inspiration and of course, lots of friendly love and affection, too. A knitters sanctuary, for sure.

Judy Paxton welcomes each guest with a hug and sincere smile, and you feel you have known this woman forever. She has knitted all her life; you immediately know this. She is very knowledgeable and helps each of her "kitting children," making her way around the table, bending to each with personal instruction and support. She loves to assist her clients in selecting the perfect yarn for their next project, and gets them started on their adventure with fiber.

"Start with a scarf," she suggests in a soft voice, "and a simple knit and purl stitch. You will soon be holding a scarf a foot long!" Oh, she is right; most ladies have an entire collection of scarves they've created here, and love to show them off, and they have all had the same endearing coach: Judy Paxton, knitter extraordinaire.

The "yarn shop ladies" gather every Tuesday and Wednesday afternoons, beginning about one o'clock, and they hang around until sometimes five, when The Art Gallery closes below. Their voices become a blurred buzz; often interrupted with shouts and loud hoots of laughter as they share their lives stories. They tell jokes, too. Time flys when you are having fun.

If you are shopping in the gallery, you will often wonder what in the world is going on up there. DD spends time in The Art Gallery helping with sales, and hears the laughter above. "Okay, you all are having just too much fun up there!" And from the loft comes even more laughter.

The ladies are very talented themselves, and all with varied backgrounds. They are mostly retired now, and from careers that would raise an eyebrow. Many are homemakers of course, but add to the group, an attorney, two doctors, an airline pilot, a commercial real estate mavin, a banker, a horse trainer, a speech therapist, a stain glass expert, and two college professors: Not too shabby for a group of knitters.

They are all accomplished artists in their own fields. They have been practicing their skills, and adding knitting to their line-up of talents for most of their lives. With each visit, they bring with them their current project to work on and for the weekly "show and tell". Close your eyes, and you can hear the "click-click-click" of knitting and weaving needles in the background as these magicians work, laugh, and chat about their daily lives outside of The Yarn Shop.

It's now four o'clock; time for Anita to leave. "Gotta catch a plane," she stands up grinning, packs up her knitting supplies and heads like Clark Kent-into-Superman, for a make-shift closet to change into her pilot uniform. Anita flies for United Airlines. Captain Anita Stanley emerges and grabs her knit bag. She heads for the stairway down, bids DD goodbye in the gallery, closing the door to the steps outside. The bell on the doorknob swings back and forth with a chime.

Upstairs, Judy shakes her head to one side and wonders to herself, "Why do they all come?"

Chapter Two

The Makers

Sometimes, Judy does not arrive until later in the afternoon, but that does not stop the ladies from getting started. When the first member arrives and grabs a chair, it is not long before a second and third join the group. They grab their needles and get down to business fast.

Some members, including Raspberry Simms, have been coming since The Yarn Shop opened and have followed Judy with her various locations in Grandville to where the shop is today. Raspberry arriving first today, is a well-known glass artist in town. She makes a living by creating and selling exquisite colorful stained glass masterpieces from her studio tucked behind her house. She's not shy: She will even help you get started on your own.

Visiting her studio on a sunny day is a must, as all of her works hang in the windows and catch the morning rays on each tiny pane, sending color in every direction. Raspberry is also an avid gardner and has the knack of combining her glass artworks with glorious flowers and trees and patios. If you are lucky, Raspberry will take you on a guided tour of her home and grounds, leaving you inspired to run out immediately and dive into your own creative adventure.

It's easy to see; color and design are Raspberry's passion. No wonder she loves helping her knitting friends select "just the right hue" and yarn texture for their own projects. Her assistance is always sought after, and so appreciated. Her specialty is to "make something from nothing." If you are invited to go trash picking with Raspberry, then do it.

You will have the time of your life, and learn something along the way, too. "Reuse and Up-cycle" is her mantra.

Raspberry heard the steps creak with a newcomer heading up the stairway.

"Geraldine! Sooooo glad to see you this afternoon! How've you been? What are you working on?"

Geraldine grabs the next chair and holds on to straighten her back. An exaggerated stretch, "Whew! Those stairs! Is this chair pour moi? Oui? Oh, tres bien!" She plopped down, grabbed her Louis Vuitton tote bag, clutching it to her chest and exhaled loudly, eyes rolling. *"Mon dieu!"* ("My God!") She was alway very dramatic. You are glad she finally found a seat.

Geraldine, the ex-realtor in the group, thinks she is French. But, she is not; she simply loves everything French, starting with the language. (She can't even pronounce that correctly most of the time.) If ever she would actually visit France, the French would be appalled at her mispronunciations and run the other way.

She loves to cook French, dine French, wear French perfume and clothes, decorate her home Country French style: you get the idea. Fleur de Lis decorator pieces consume every surface. Very over-done. Feeds her fru-fru dog (yes, a poodle named Francois) French bread or croutons. Always has a French manicure. Her favorite color is French Blue. But of course. Sometimes, she drives the ladies crazy with all of her French talk, but they love her joy, spontaneity, and melodrama. What a character.

She really is entertaining. They love to tease, asking her "When is she is going to France" for the next trip. This guarantees them another lesson in faulty French.

"Ooh, La La! I have so many projects going on, *Je suis dizzy!*" Geraldine is a new knitter, always in a panic, always asking for help, with all the members gladly providing the assistance needed to finish each project.

She is currently working on her fourth scarf, with a French flair ruffle, but of course. She has a system with her many projects: Geraldine works each one until she experiences a problem like slipped stitches, and then returns it to her tote bag until she meets again with her knitter friends and they can help her out of her bind. Today, she has carried not one, but three projects for them to untangle for her. Gotta love Geraldine. She keeps trying.

The group expands as Marna and Sandy arrive. Unlike Geraldine, Marna really IS European; being born in Holland. Even though she has lived in the U.S for many years, she still has a heavy Dutch accent, and is asked often about her home country. She has a hard time pronouncing the "th" sound, as in "thanks," so it always comes out "tanks," or "I tink it is dis way."

People gravitate to Marna and her warm personality. Maybe it's because of her charming accent; maybe it's because of her generosity, but you just want to be near her. She is wise as an owl with good common sense advise for all, and above all, she is believable. Sometimes mysterious, but believable, nonetheless.

Marna is an accomplished knitter and crochet master, proudly wearing each week, one of her many accomplishments, each one exquisite. Today she is working on a sweater coat for her daughter, and her fellow knitters are in awe. She is always perky, sits very straight in her chair with good posture.

Marna has a dry sense of humor which sometimes catches the other members off guard. She swims everyday; wears her curly silver gray hair natural due to the pool chlorine. The epitome of good health and clean living, Marna has many admirers. Maybe it's those little black licorice Dutch candies she is always eating. She plunks the bag on the table.

"I brought tees to share," offering her sweets to all. Geraldine and Sandy take one; Raspberry passes. They munch away, and pretty soon, Sandy gets up unexpectedly and heads downstairs to use the restroom, in which she quickly and secretly spits out the little black sour treat.

"Yuck!" Sandy gets a glass of water and returns upstairs to join the group. She is recently widowed, and the members are quick to support her with positive topics to discuss and keep her focused on the project at hand, which is not knitting, but hooking.

She loves to announce, " I am a hooker!" just to get a rise from any audience. Currently Sandy is making a rug for her new RV, which she has just bought all by herself, which should tell you a little bit about Sandy . Talk about independent. She shares her story of purchasing her new "rig", all by herself and driving it to her first rally "with the group." Each week, the members get an update on Sandy's travels. This month was to the Dallas NASCAR event at The Texas Motor Speedway.

"That's over three hundred miles!" The ladies stop knitting and stare at Sandy. They are mesmerized. Who knows where Sandy will be headed this winter. Sometimes the ladies are stunned, and have no words to respond to these adventures; but secretly, they all wish they could be a little more like Sandy.

Joining in next was Katy Smith, known for her experience in "living rural." In Texas, that means ranch. She lives farthest from the Yarn Shop; her drive is a long one; yet she never complains. Katy is one of those women other women envy: lives beyond the fringe....Does her own thing, not explaining anything to anybody.

A natural beauty, who grows more beautiful with each year. How does this happen? She wears nearly no make-up, and yet looks as though she just had a facial. (What does she use, anyway?) Always wearing beautiful silver jewelry with her hair pulled straight back (her gray strands are just perfect), she captures all of the attention with her "horse stories" from the ranch. Sit there for a while at the table: Just by listening to Katy each week, you can learn just about anything done on a ranch, from cattle to chickens; from feed to poop.

And that's not all. Katy is also a garden expert; a Certified Master Gardener who works three days a week managing the local nursery, providing expertise about perennials and annuals, and where to plant (or not to plant) a prized Japanese maple. People come from all over just to ask her about their plants and talk dirt and fertilizer. She will provide the recipe for the perfect recycled compost for any who ask. Katy is "Mother Nature" sitting at your side.

Raspberry helps Katy with the selection of yarns for a special "dreadlocks" handbag she wants to make. The ladies lean over look in Katy's knitting magazine at the photo of the finished bag. They pass it around the table.

"Oh My God, that's gorgeous!" shouts Judy, as she enters her own shop. "When are you going to start on this?"

"As soon as I finish this scarf!" laughs Katy, then they are on to the next subject, only to be interrupted by Mary Ellen Afton taking the last available chair that day.

Mary Ellen is a spinner. Meaning, her craft is the expert talent of taking raw fiber, from either a sheep, or an alpaca, or a goat, and carding it to a consistency that can be spun either on a spinning wheel, or a drop spinner spindle, which looks like a child's small top.

Mary Ellen gives lessons on these techniques, if you are interested, at The Yarn Shop. She picked up a drop spindle and began.

Watching Mary Ellen spin is mesmerizing. Working together, her hands move very little, but the spindle becomes a blur and the ball of fuzz suddenly becomes a beautiful strand of yarn which she winds into a ball. Watch her spin too long, and you will get dizzy.

This skill is very contagious, as once you begin your adventure with fiber, it's only a matter of time before you evolve from knitter to spinner. Like knitting, spinning is very sedentary: You sit very still and you don't move around a lot.

Mary Ellen has told the ladies how she often has fallen "asleep at the wheel," at her big Spinner and fallen on the floor!

Marna looked across the table at her friend, spinning away. "Hmmmmm......Hello? Mary Ellen! Earth to Mary Ellen! Come back to us!"

The table is full. Everyone is chatting and the needles are singing. Someone pours the coffee, and just then, Geraldine's eyes dart to the middle of the table. She noticed an adorable little stuffed toy furry rat peaking from several balls of mohair yarn and knitting needles.

It was a little girl rat, very dainty, and only about six inches tall. Her fur was a soft tan color, like a fawn, with shiny black eyes. She was wearing a light multi-colored pink crocheted dress and matching hat with a little flower on it, and she held a tiny little teddy bear in her arms! Her eyes twinkled in the light, and she looked like she had something to say.

Geraldine pick up the little girl rat, and with a scream of excitement said, "Oh how cute is that! She even has panties! Whose little raet is this, and where did she come from?"

Judy piped up, "If you mean 'rat,' then that's Chloe, and I made her myself! And I also made her tiny teddy bear! Isn't she beautiful?"

How could anyone make such a perfect little animal? Raspberry explained to everyone that teddy-bear making was one of Judy's specialties. "She's teddy-bear famous!" For years, she had crafted many bears, and now teaches classes. Judy leaned forward and looked at her friends. "You know, if you can make a bear, you can make a rat."

And that's where the REAL RAT STORY begins.

Chapter Three

Rats

Everyone turned to the middle of the table to look at Chloe. They stopped knitting, and all eyes were focused on the little fur rodent perched on a fluff of yellow yarn.

Geraldine picked up Chloe again examining her very closely. Before her career in real estate, she used to sew professionally and recognized how intricate the stitches were and the skills involved in her creation. She inspected every inch of the rat, recognizing the perfection of craftsmanship, then carefully set Chloe back down on the table and looked directly at Judy. "OK, I want to make one of these!"

Marna was equally impressed with the little rat. Even though she was the crochet champion of the group, she was eager, too. "If Geraldine makes one, I want to make one too, and dey can be pals!"

Judy turned, disappeared behind the shelves and returned with three more rats, and lovingly assembled them next to Chloe. "These are my babies!"

She was so proud. Holding each one up for all to see, she introduced everyone each rat and the knitters passed them around in wonder. They turned them around in their hands for inspection.

Each toy rat was very different: there were girl rats, and boy rats; some wore fancy clothes of the city with coats and hats, and some were obviously country rats! Some were even a little shabby, as if they had a hard life. These must have been poor! Some were chubby and made a little larger; some were smaller and dainty. Their faces expressed a different feeling. But for sure, *every rat was unique and had its own personality.*

Judy beamed. "These little toy rats are very special, and no two are alike. I order their mohair fur from Germany, and it takes many weeks to make just one rat, as there are so many steps involved."

Judy smiled, and picked up a very shaggy one, kind of rusty in color, wearing a colorful knitted hat and matching scarf. "This one is Ratcliff"! DD made her. "Isn't she adorable?"

There was another, named Lenny, wearing a blue plaid vest and cap, who would find a home with her oldest grandson, whose name was also Lenny, for Christmas.

Another tan colored shaggy fir rat, with soft purple "skin" was named Violet. She had the funniest eyes; they were sewn closer together, so they looked like they were almost crossed. Violet looked like she might have tipped a few. Judy said she made Violet in memory of her Grandmother, who liked to indulge in wines.

"When Grandma was asked if she wanted a refill, her favorite response was 'Just enough to wet my lips!" Wild hoots of laughter filled the room. Everyone just stared. They all were wide-eyed, with their mouths open, holding their hands close to their chins with awe.

Sandy wanted to know more about their fur coats. "What *is* mohair, anyway?"

DD came up the stairs, hearing the buzz. "Mohair comes from Angora goats," she said. "They are only raised in Texas; their angora coats are shaved, and the angora is then sent to Germany, where it is carded and processed into mohair. Remember those teddy bears from your childhood? The really good ones were made by Steiff. They were made in Germany; and they still make them today."

The knitters were petting all of the rat fir coats now, hanging on to every word. Each was holding a rat for inspection. DD continued, "Judy and I have made our teddy bears for years; now we make the rats in the same format as these famous bears from Germany."

You could hear a pin drop. The knitters were spellbound.

Judy could see they were all impressed. She looked at all the ladies, whose eyes were glued to her rat collection. Quietly, almost a whisper to all at the table, "Would you like to make one? We can start a rat class, and you can make your own rat!"

Well, there were no second thoughts. Everyone loved the idea of making their very own rat. This would be a new adventure they couldn't resist, and they couldn't wait to sign up.

Raspberry picked up Chloe. "This is the cutest thing I have ever seen!" Turning her over for closer inspection, she marveled at her fuzzy body. You couldn't even see the stitches. "Look at her bright shiny eyes and her tiny feet and arms!" Chloe had soft little ears, and her curly tail was made of smooth leather. Her arms and legs and head all moved and turned at the touch. She turned Chloe's head towards her, and gazed into her eyes. All the rats looked *so very real.* "Count me in!" she said.

Mary Ellen chimed in. "Their whiskers and eyelashes *were* real, as they were made from real strands of horse tail hair." Jaws dropped. Mary Ellen continued, "The horse strands actually came from my horses, and when they are groomed, I collect some very good samples and bring them to Judy for rat making." She held up a plastic ziplock bag loaded with horse hair.

"Holy Cow!" Marna was astonished, and she was hooked. Rosemary gently returned Chloe to her spot on the table. "Count me in, too!" she confirmed.

It was settled, then. Geraldine, Raspberry, Sandy, Marna, Mary Ellen, and Katy would form the "first rat class" at the Yarn Shop. They would become rat makers extraordinaire, and create six rats to join the four sitting on the table in front of them. Soon, there would be ten little rats in Grandville, Texas.

Judy confirmed, "We will begin next Tuesday, at eleven o'clock, and everyone bring your lunch. It's gonna be a long day!"

Then, it was back to the projects of the day, with the rats taking center stage on the table. Each of the ladies picked up her needles and began projects, but the buzz of conversation was all about the rats.
They were pumped. Judy asked, "Geraldine, how do you say, 'rat' in French?"

"*C'est facilite!* Its' simple! Rat, in French is very similar and sounds the same: "*raet!*" and ours will be *les petite raets de Grandville!* The Little Rats of Grandville! *Tres*

Bien!" And with that, she picked up her Louis Vuitton tote bag, stuffed her knitting needles, half-finished scarf number four (with a French ruffle, of course) inside, jumped up from her chair and with a flourish that always caught everyone's attention, headed for the stairs. THINKING ABOUT HER RAT. *Au revoir, mes amies!*

Chapter Four

Rat Days

Anita Stanley was the first to arrive on the first Rat Day Tuesday. What a shock. She had no idea her knitter friends had gone completely nuts, and jumped from knitting into making rats. She found a seat and brought her knit project to the table. Anita could hear the chatter and excitement below.

As the ladies arrived, they were talking at the same time about their new project. You could hear the buzz across the street!

Anita placed a beautiful tin of tea cookies in the middle of the table. She had just returned from a flight to Belgium, and always brought something exotic from her travels to share. Listening to the conversation, she looked up and very cautiously asked, "What do you mean, you are making ra-a-a-ts?"

Raspberry plopped down with her knitting bag, grabbed the closest chair and explained the hubbub.

"I guess we have all gone crazy, but last week we all fell in love with these little guys!" Huffing and puffing with her entrance, "I know we are going to have a really good time making these!" She pointed to the furry group sitting in the middle of yarn puffs on the table. "Just look at these little things!"

Anita picked up Violet and Chloe and began to inspect. "Wow!" She was mesmerized. "Aren't these cute!"

The stairway steps creaked as you could hear the rest of the Rat Pack slowly making their way up, nearly bumping into each other to find their seats. A cacophony of chatter.

Everyone was talking at the same time as Geraldine snuck in a seat right next to Judy. Looking over her shoulder directly at the teacher, "I want to get everything just right," she said.

Now they were assembled and ready to start. Next to Judy and Geraldine was Raspberry; then came Marna, Sandy, Katy, Mary Ellen, and now, across from Marna was Anita, who was nodding excitedly, "Yes, Yes!" and ready to join the group.

Nine rat makers all together: The Original Rat Pack all lined up like chipmunks, sitting with their paws up and their teeth showing; very eager, and ready to start.

They were all so excited about making their own rat. Each had a plan and a story in her head about the little furry personality they would create, as they had thought about it all week long.

As the friends talked about their own rat, they became more familiar with the furs, the leather for their feet, ears, and tails. Soon, and with much love, each of these little rats would have a different look and begin to develop individual personalities of their own.

Judy brought out a big box of fur samples, and explained why the fur was very special.
"You can't just go to the store and buy this kind of fur. Remember, these pieces all came from Germany, they are very expensive, and each fur is unique; as some are curly,

and some are even kind of shaggy," she said. "Take your time. You just have to pick out just the right fur you like best for your own rat."

The box was passed around. Each held up fur pieces, touching them to their cheeks, petting the nap with their hands, and soon, everyone had the fur and leather pieces they wanted. "I like this one," and, "this one is perfect for me!"

And so, in The Yarn Shop loft, the rat making process began, and Rat Makers were born.

The click of the knitting needles was replaced with the sounds of fur being laid out, measured, and cut. The Rat Pack worked with such energy that first day, laying out patterns for legs and arms and bodies on their fur. Feet and arms and a long tail would be cut from soft leather. So real. All day, they worked.

The clock in the corner ticked away; sometimes it was the only sound heard, but most of the time the Makers were talking loudly and laughed about "their great rat adventure upstairs in The Yarn Shop" and how their lives changed from the moment the friends sat down together. They were joyful together. Sheer bliss. No stress. No problems. Not to worry about their diet, their hair do. There wasn't even any gossip. Just smile, laugh, relax, and make a rat.

Shoppers downstairs in the art gallery looked up at the table of women chatting and laughing in the loft above.
"Wonder what in the world they are doing up there! said someone below. Oh, if they only knew.

It was intricate work. Judy showed each of the Makers how to clip the fur correctly. "You have to snip gently with

33

the points of the scissors; do not cut the fur, so the nap will lay properly," she said.

And so, as they clipped and snipped, imaginations raced ahead in high speed. You could almost hear the concentration. Everyone began telling each other about their own rat, as they each seemed to already have a story.

Geraldine, always animated, announced her rat was a boy, and he had a name already. "He will be known as 'Pierre, and he will only speak French! He will have a mustache, wear a French beret, and he will love all the lady rats!" Of course.

Everyone laughed, knowing Geraldine would choose a French name. But they all were surprised to hear about her rat's personality, as well. Geraldine had him all figured out.

Judy picked up on this. "When Pierre was all finished, he would probably fall in love with her beautiful little rat, Chloe!" She thought for a moment and wanted to know, "How would Pierre be able to talk to the other rats if he only speaks French?"

"Oh, Pierre will give French lessons to all the other rats in the shop at night when they are all alone, of course," responded Geraldine with no hesitation; confident that her Pierre could do whatever he wanted. After all, he was French, you know.

"And then, all of The Yarn Shop rats can communicate in Rat-French at night!"

Laughter ran around the table.

"Oh my God." Eyes rolling, Marna popped one of her licorice candies into her mouth. She held her fluffy gray rat up like a puppet, and "made" him talk to Pierre and Raspberry. "What do you tink my name should be, do you tink? How about 'Fluffy'?"

Pierre jumped up, thanks to a title help from Geraldine. *"Absolutement, non!"* said Pierre. *"C'est tres ennuyeux!"* (Geraldine reminded everyone Pierre only speaks French, and that the name "Fluffy" was boring.)

Well, Marna's rat name would be something spectacular, then. "All right, I will name him after an old boyfriend of mine, who seemed very nice at first and he was very handsome, but turned out to be A REAL RAT! He was very mysterious. I never did find out what he did in the underworld; he would never tell me the truth. His name will be Antonius LeBeau, but I will call him 'Le Beau," for short."

"Tres bien!" cheered Pierre. "What about your rat, Raspberry? What will it be? Boy? Girl? Name?"

Raspberry was very cool. She slowly stood up, placed her hand on the table, then leaned over and looked directly into Geraldine's eyes. Then she pushed her rat across the slick surface towards Pierre. "SHE will be known as 'Rattina,' that's with two 't's', and she will be extremely gifted in the arts!"

Well, knowing Raspberry and her talent, no one was surprised she would come up with a cultural rat.

Geraldine said, "A painter, no less! She will probably carry a paint brush and a palette around with her!" But, of course.

That gave Raspberry an idea......She returned to her sitting position and finished another detail on Rattina. "Maybe a tiara?" she thought.

Everyone was now on a roll. The rats were taking shape, and their names and personalities were being formed. Clip, clip, clip. The sheets of fur and leather formed the legs and arms and bodies of every little rat. Each of the Makers took a turn, introducing her rat to the members of this crazy group.

Sandy was so excited, "I was watching the Today Show last week, and they were in Madrid. They were talking about the most famous mouse in Spain, and guess what? He is 'El Ratoncito Perez,' the Spanish equivalent of our Tooth Fairy!" Sandy went on. "As best I can tell, he takes children's baby teeth, leaves money under the pillow, and then turns the teeth into pearls!"

Everybody stopped clipping and looked at Sandy. Mary Ellen was curious. "What does the rat do with the pearls?"

"Well, nobody knows, I guess." Sandy continued, "The Today Show didn't take it any farther than that, and then, you know, they break for a commercial, and that was that." She hesitated, thinking. "I think I will go online, see what I can find out" But for now she held up her little fur rat, sans stuffing. He just dangled in her hands.

"Meet my own little 'El Ratoncito Perez,' sans pearls!"

Mary Ellen stood up. "Oh, Great! What an international group of Rats! Looks like we have the entire world represented here, except the great state of Texas! I think mine better be a local from Fort Worth...or somewhere out west, but I need more time." She started picking up her work area. "Hmmmmm... A Texan, fer shure!"

It was getting late, and the group was getting tired. The Art Shop below had closed two hours ago. All that rat-naming takes a lot of energy. Time for the Rat Pack to call it a day and pack it up.

Katy hugged Mary Ellen and announced she would be ready with a name next week, too. With that, everyone packed up their half-finished rats and supplies.

Geraldine picked up Pierre, kissed him on both cheeks, European style and gently tucked him in her Louis Vuitton bag (of course), and they all gave each other hugs and goodbyes until next time. Then, with a flourish and a wave, *"Au revoir, mes Amiees!"* Life in the Yarn Shop was good.

Chapter Five

Rat Pals

When one becomes an official Rat Maker, one suddenly becomes obsessed with the little thing. Rats are all they think about, talk about, and they seem to feel compelled to describe their adventure with friends and family. This is confirmed between the Rat Pack members when they start to describe their conversations with the outside world.

Following that first session, the Makers found themselves telling everyone they knew "they were making a rat, and waited for the expression of their listener. The responses were hysterical. In almost every case, it was the same: "What do you MEAN, YOU ARE MAKING A RAT!" and, "YOU MEAN A REAL RAT?" and, "ARE YOU KIDDING ME!" and, "WHAT KIND OF RAT, EXACTLY?"

The attention the Makers received was overwhelming. Nobody had paid them any mind when they talked about knitting and crocheting. Ho-Hum. Yawn. But now, things were different. Really different. OH, yeah... Rats!

Now they were STARS! Now they were interesting! Family members and friends either listened with keen interest and wanted to hear more, or they thought their crazy friend had finally gone over the edge. The Makers all began to look forward to a discussion with anybody that would listen about their new adventure in rat making. They were all close to obnoxious!

Grandville is one of the many "Texas County seat" towns, where the middle of town boasts a registered historic stone court house with parking spaces all around it.

Very park-like. Some have historical monuments denoting famous Texans standing in front. A tidy collection of retail shops usually ring the court house, forming a "downtown square."

If you live in Grandville, you simply refer to the historic downtown as "The Square." It's a town with character. The buildings are old but pristine; each one different, and many constructed from Texas Hill Country River rock called "Grandville stone." Architects come from all over to study and copy the building designs.

If you think about it, Grandville's Square is like a Monopoly game for real and women of all ages flock here to "go around and shop the square" passing "GO" many times, and purchasing as much as they can along the way. Unfortunately, unless they stop at the corner bank, they do not "collect $200" each time around. Just replace the four railroads with gift shop boutiques, and exchange St. James Place for apparel shops, add a couple of bistros where you would see Park Place and the Boardwalk, and there you have it: A perfect collection of retail shops and restaurants where you can park easy, walk around in an afternoon, say hello to your friends, and have a nice lunch at the Tea House.

The Square is shopping heaven, and ladies from all over Texas come by the busload. Tour busses line up in parking lots all around the back of the shops.

Oh, the drivers here are polite. They have to be! They always know to stop for any lady with a shopping bag or two strapped to her shoulder, as she will most likely be with another friend, leaning in to each other in excited conversation; completely oblivious to any traffic around her. If they stop to see the driver, they of course wave "thank you." They are very courteous.

In the park, there are many benches for patient husbands to wait for their expert shopper- wives, too.

It's a wonderful place. If you are just driving through, you tell yourself, "Someday I will come back here to live." Everyone loves Grandville.

It was Rat Day Tuesday at The Yarn Shop. Autumn had retained some of summer's warm temperatures, and the fall days in Texas were mild enough for just a light shawl or scarf. Cold in the mornings, but by noon the sun was out to warm your back, and the sky was bright blue. Made your eyes squint, so sun glasses were a must. The perfect fall day.

They began arriving. One by one, and toting their project bags, eagerly the Rat Makers waived to each other, and hurriedly made their way from the parking lot across the street, and upstairs to The Yarn Shop. What a hustle.

The Art Gallery is a Victorian style building, with a gingerbread rooftop trim; the only white building on the street. It faces east and captures the sun, so in the mornings upon opening, the building stands out much brighter than the rest of the retail lineup on First Street.

The door was most likely the original one from the early twentieth century, complete with a little brass doorknob with a bell chime that turns very easily in your hand. You push the door inward to enter, and you never know who

41

might greet you among the art pieces, gifts, and jewelry upon entry.

Samantha, the owner, has many volunteers who help in the shop. This was a place you just wanted to be involved and surround yourself with art; no pay was necessary. Just to be there was enough.

She watched with wonder as one by one, the Rat Pack began to assemble in the loft. Samantha had never heard such chatter upstairs.

"Is knitting really that exciting?" she wondered.

Early bird Katy was already in her seat talking about her rat (she wouldn't tell anybody her rat's name until the group was all there) when the rest of the pack made their way up the stairs. Oh, were they excited.

They all knew they were on to something special, and couldn't wait to get started.

With Mary Ellen, followed by Marna and Geraldine, they only had to wait for Raspberry, Anita, Sandy, and the owners Judy and DD, who were on their way.

Within ten minutes, they were all assembled, seated, armed with scissors in their hands. The excitement was contagious, and circled the table. What a group. No need for too much small talk today; The Rat Pack was vibrating and ready to go.

Judy and DD were very proud of their new little group of rat makers. Judy looked at Katy. "Well, don't keep us in suspense; tell us about your rat!"

Katy smiled widely making sure she had everyone's attention and announced her rat was a little girl gardener rat named "Echo". She was going to be very green, very environmental: "The rat recycle Princess!" Katy planned to make her clothes from reworked something; she didn't know what just yet, but they would be green, naturally. Everyone agreed, this was the perfect rat for Katy; and as you recall, she was also known as "Mother Nature" in the group.

That left DD, and Mary Ellen, and they were ready to tell all. DD, her talent not to be outdone by anyone, said she was making three rats.

"My three little girl rats are the 'Southern Belles.' They are sisters; Bella, Beauty, and Bonnie, (BBB!) and they will live in the Southern end of the Yarn Shop. They will like all things sweet, and especially praline pecan pie," she said matter of faculty.

"Et Les hommes, naturalement!" (And the men, naturally!), interrupted Geraldine.

Praline pecan pie was DD's favorite. She liked to make it for guests, even when it wasn't a special holiday. This gave her the opportunity to eat the remainder in the pie pan when everyone had left. Nice little secret.

Always neat as a pin. Fashion conscious: always dressed to the max. Perfect makeup. Current hair style: right now a soft blonde bob. Striking. And her clothes! (she always shopped the Square to support her fellow merchants), and don't forget: nothing was complete without her teddy bear jewelry.

43

DD always had something teddy bear on, denoting her special bear making skills, in case anyone needed instruction on how to make a teddy bear, they knew who to ask. A born marketer, these pieces always created interest, and a great opening conversation.

"I'm making Bella first, and she will be the all-time rat fashion queen." DD's stitches were meticulous, and her little rat Bella, was perfectly made. Very delicate, made of a soft peach colored fur, and a little smaller than the rest of the rats, which meant her seams were a little wider .

Bella was already quite the looker in the group, and just like her Maker, was beautiful. (Just wait till she makes her clothes!)

Mary Ellen was last, but not least. She had been listening to everyone, and remembered the comments made last week about the need for a "local rat." So no surprise, she would create TEX, and he will "keep the peace in the rat neighborhood." Sheriff TEX, no less.

Born and raised in Forth Worth; Texas, we are talkin' NATIVE. He would sport a leather vest, wear the Texas star, and tip his Texas Stetson hat to the ladies. Talk about a true Texan rat. "Howdy, y'all!" You git the ideee-a. She had to find him boots somewhere.

Oh, this was good. There was a French rat named Pierre, who only spoke French, an artist rat named Rattina, who had a flair for color and textures, a Dutch rat named LeBeau, whose morals were quite questionable and mysterious, a tooth-fairy-type named El Ratoncito Perez who galavanted about in the night (for what we may never know).

Echo, the naturalist recycled "green queen," the three Southern Belles, who lived in the South end of the store (that would be Bella, Beauty, and Bonnie) who would most likely have an affection for anything pecan, and all of these would join the original rats; Chloe, Lenny, Violet and Ratcliff.

And they would all be kept in line by a bonafide Texan Sheriff rat from Fort Worth.

Lots of chatter and screams, now.

The Makers were nearly hysterical, laughing with tears in their eyes and trying to remember all the names, and trying to get their personalities all straight.

They suddenly stopped laughing, wiped their eyes and stared at each other wide-eyed with their mouths open.

They knew it now, their rats were just like themselves. How and why did they do this? It just happened. Magically. They were giddy with delight. Thirteen rats in all.

Suddenly, from the art shop below, came a shout.

"WAIT! Don't leave out Sir Reginald!" It was Samantha, who owned The Art Gallery. She had a rat, too! Judy had forgotten: she had made a rat for Samantha many months ago as a special surprise "thank you" gift for all Samantha had done for her.

Not being a knitter, Samantha was never seen at the gathering table, as she was always involved with her own art, and hers was a talent unlike any of the knitters. When she was not in her glass blowing studio, or on the sales floor and talking with customers about her work, she was in the back room on accounting days, keeping her books straight and sending emails.

She was very serious, and unbeknown to all, very superstitious. Was afraid of black cats. Samantha never stepped on cracks, walked under ladders, and she always stayed home on Friday the Thirteenth.

She loved Sir Reginald, who sat on top of her printer for good luck. His job was to make sure the copies always came out okay, and that the printer did not screw something up.

He was a loner; but not by choice. He just didn't know what in the heck was going on up in the loft. So Sir Reginald made up "number fourteen; not Thirteen.

Thank goodness. They counted and recounted: Fourteen very unique rats were now underway in The Yarn Shop in Grandville, Texas. Sir Reginald. Lucky Fourteen.

Chapter Six

Making a Rat

As Grandville's fall days grew colder, the Makers became stronger with their mission. The sky turned grayer, the sun was not seen for days sometimes, and still the Makers came; totally dedicated, they never missed Rat Day Tuesday together at The Yarn Shop.

Foot traffic in the shops on The Square weakened to just a few shoppers and those that came were only "lookers" searching for next-to nothing bargain deals. Just before the holidays, yet! Several Rat Days came and went, and the process of making rats was slow but purposeful.

The Makers were unusually focused. Everyone let their numerous knitting and weaving projects go by the wayside; the rats were the main thing in their lives right now. Rat making was serious business and nothing else much mattered.

You might say, "They were crazed."

As they cut, sewed, and stuffed, the Makers talked about their rat's personalities. They began to share more about their personal lives outside The Yarn shop, and if you watched and listened closely, you could see they slowly wove themselves into their own little furry friends.

Geraldine spoke more French, and so did Pierre.

Marna's early years in Holland revealed a more secretive life and Le Beau became a little more mysterious with his questionable background.

Raspberry made Rattina "talk," and the rat's "art advise" was sought after by every rat maker, and this sometimes caused a disturbance with the other rats as everybody had their own opinion to share.

This initiated the "talking" of the rats by each Maker, and they all started holding up their rats like puppets.

Mary Ellen walked her rat across the table. She would have to ask Sheriff TEX to step in and control the lot. "Okay, everybody jist simmer down!" TEX shouted. And then there was peace on the rat table.

They were nearly all finished. This Tuesday was "eye day," and each was to select the set of eyes she wanted for her rat. This took time, as eyes were very important. Judy instructed, "If you place them too high, your rat will look old, and if you place them too low, your rat will look young!" she passed around a small box of rat eyeballs.

They all tested their rat eyes in different positions. Judy was right!

Geraldine placed Pierre's eyes dead-center, brought him up close to her, looked him straight in the eyes with her own and announced, *"Il parfait!"* Perfect!
But of course.

The rats had all different colored eyes, and some of the Makers learned to highlight her rat eyes with a bit of white felt, so the rat seemed to be looking up or down. The felt gave them even more personality. Le Beau's eyes were always looking down, so he looked like he was keeping some dark secret. Sheriff TEX looked straight ahead, letting all know "who was running the show." There was no question about this rat.

Arms and legs were attached to bodies and joints installed, so that all limbs and the head would turn, just like a human. This was an intricate procedure. There were two essential pieces for each joint: a very hard wood-like disc with a hole in the middle, and a cotter-key piece that connected the disc. They shared special pliers to do the job, and some of the Maker's arthritic hands had trouble, so another Maker with some real strength would step in to help. "Hummmp! There you go!" Everyone breathed a sighs of relief when all the joints were in and arms and legs and heads all moved.

They wiggled their rats arms and legs and turned the heads around to test each joint. Wonderful! They all worked. They all moved about just like a human. The Makers moved the limp rats around the table in front of them to introduce each other. They seemed to greet each other! "Howdy, M'am!" Sheriff TEX said to Rattina, who just turned her head and blushed.

"Okay ladies, now we stuff!" With an air of pride, Judy pulled out a large bag of stuffing.

"Now listen everybody, take just a teeny bit of stuffing at a time; and I mean a tiny bit, and poke it inside your rat, then use a pointed pencil to push it inside all the way to the foot, and then, PACK IT HARD!" She made her way around the table, checking each rat.

Even though they tried, nobody stuffed their rat hard enough. Judy picked up each rat, tested for hardness, touched the end of the foot, squeezed the hand, and returned the rat to its Maker.

"Harder," She said, then on to the next in line. "Sorry, a little harder," handing the creature back.

Some of the rat makers got a little miffed.

"Isn't this okay?"

"I kind of like mine a little soft in the middle."

This was totally unacceptable. Judy said. "They wouldn't sit up or stand right and you want them to be strong, you know." So, bit by bit, the stuffing session went on. Stuff and pack, and push the pencil, stuff and pack, push the pencil, and by the end of the day, the rats took shape.

Just before they finished stuffing, Judy and DD looked at each other, then smiling from ear to ear, announced they had a surprise for everyone. DD excused herself from the table and returned with a very small satin red and pink box in the shape of a heart. She held it up for all to see.

"What....?????" thought everyone. Valentine's Day was still months away, so what was this? DD opened the box, and poured out a bunch of tiny red crocheted hearts on the table that she and Judy had made for each Maker to place inside their rat.

Judy leaned forward and picked up a heart and held it up. "Now your rats will all have a heart and soul. They can feel the love you've all given them!"

The Makers were amazed, and very grateful. How thoughtful. What a kind and tender gesture for their teachers to do. The hearts were passed around. Each Maker picked up a heart and tenderly placed it deep inside their rat with their finger, and then without saying a word, they quietly sewed up the back seam. You could hear a pin drop in The Yarn Shop.

The Makers set their rats down and looked back and forth at each other. My goodness, were they all happy, or what? The rats were sewn, and everyone glanced about the table checking rat status. Marna held her rat up for all to see, tilted her head for opinions. She liked to repeat her questions, "What do you tink, do you tink?"

Anita commented, "LeBeau is so handsome! Was the real LeBeau this good looking?"

Marna confirmed, "Oh my, yes! Yes! How do you tink I fell for him so easily? But ten, he lef me. Gone. Just lef wit no word for me. What a scoundrel rat he became!" Anita said, " LeBeau is Dutch, and Pierre is French. They will most likely become great friends as we all are."

Marna's mind drifted somewhere. She didn't say anymore and gently sat LeBeau back on the table quite satisfied with herself.

She focused on the other rats, all now stuffed, with eyes starring back at her. "We done, I tink!" She pulled out a licorice candy.

With exception of clothes and hats, and a few last-minute finishes like whiskers and eyebrows, the rats were complete.

Raspberry asked, "I suppose LeBeau will like that black licorice candy just like you do, too?"

Marna answered back with only a smile. "I bet you are right, I tink!" She pulled out another piece of her candy and put it on the table right in front of LeBeau. "Dare! Enjoy yourself; my little Dutch rat!"

Raspberry, resident artist in Grandville, was the last to finish that day. She had taken extra time and thought with her fur selection, which was actually a little scruffy (texture, you know). She was slow to select the perfect color for eyes and then had to find special yarn for a scarf she planned to make later for Rattina.

Before they knew it, the day was complete, and so were the rats. There, in front of them and lovingly placed in the center of the table amongst the balls of yarn sat the rats:

Geraldine's Pierre
Marna's LeBeau
Raspberry's Rattina
Sandy's El Ratoncito Perez
Katy's Echo
Mary Ellen's Sheriff TEX

The first of DD's three Southern Belles, Bella, was sitting next to Anita's rat, but Anita had trouble with a name for her little furry friend. Everyone offered suggestions, but none really hit on the button.

Her rat was dark sable brown, with wide eyes and a warm and confident smile. At this point, her rat could be a boy or a girl; as without eye lashes yet, or whiskers, or other finishing touches; you just couldn't be sure.

Anita said, "I need another week just to be sure," and with that she quickly scooped up her creation and held it close to her chest. You could tell she was not sharing her thoughts on this just yet.

Judy disappeared for a moment, then returned with Chloe, Lenny, Violet, and Ratcliff, and placed them with their new friends. There were now thirteen rats on the table.

Everyone beamed. Never, in a million years, would any of them thought they would become Rat Makers Extraordinaire.

They looked lovingly at the collection before them. They all had heart and soul. They all looked completely different and had personalities of their own and they were dearly loved by the ladies who made them. These, they knew, they would never sell, or even give them away. As that would be giving away a piece of themselves.

It was time to go home. The Makers were tired, but it was a "good tired." They were exhausted and sat limp in their seats. A couple were even breathing hard. "Whew! What a day!"

Judy looked at the rats on the table. "My gosh, what an accomplishment!" she said. Rather than pack them up and take them home, She suggested, "Why don't we leave the rats on the table for all her other customers to see and admire. Maybe there will be other ladies who will want to make a rat!"

What a great idea! Everyone agreed. This was an excellent marketing plan on Judy's part. The rats looked right at home on the table, and very happy.

Anita thought out loud, "Maybe we can start a rat club, or something." Judy reached out and arranged the little fur people on the balls of yarn. "Oh, you ALREADY are a rat club! QUITE a rat club!"

They all laughed. Rat Makers Extraordinare! But of course!

DD looked at the rats, then she remembered. "Oh, don't forget Sir Reginald, who lives downstairs in the art gallery." She counted in her head: "He makes fourteen rats...."

"That's right," said Sandy. "Remember, he takes care of things for Samantha from his perch on the printer."

"God help us all if we didn't have Sir Reginald!"

The makers felt sorry Sir Reginald was alone down there. "Should we bring him up and add him to the group?" asked Raspberry.

DD shook her head. "Oh no, remember? Samantha needs him for good luck?"

With that, the ladies gathered up their tote bags, cleaned up the work area in front of them, said goodbye to their little rat friends, and headed for the stairway down. Goodbyes, and hugs to each other.

"See you next week for the final touches!" They were all out the door and across the street to the parking lot.

It was a wrap: Another Rat Day under the table. A big day.

Judy thought about her weeks with these ladies: Her Makers. The little bits of fur she had kept in a box tucked away in the back room had become a tidy group of fourteen little rat souls made with pride and love, each very different, and each with a very unique personality. Just like the ladies who made them.

The knitters who originally came to just knit and purl together for an afternoon of polite conversation had become loving friends who created something as crazy as a furry little rat that would bind them in life forever.

The clock tower on the top of the court house struck six o'clock. It was late.

Dark and quiet now in the shop already. Judy doused the lights up in the loft, and holding the rail extra tight, balancing a large collection of yarns and supplies, slowly made her way down the stairway alone with extra caution.

She glanced up into the loft and looked up at the rats still visible in the dim light on the table. "Night- night little guys," she said softly, then, turned out the last light in the gallery, and closed the door shut. All was very quiet. Or was it?

Chapter Seven

Something Amiss

Judy parked her car in front of The Yarn Shop. She had her pick of spaces today as it was Sunday and always a slow day for business. With football games on TV and the rain coming down outside it was a perfect day for her to catch up in her shop.

Rat making days had dominated her time away from other knitting projects, and she needed to inventory her supplies, not to mention give the place a good dusting and a reorganization of the shop in general.

Sales were not would they should be these days and she knew she and DD had to do whatever it took to keep the whole thing going. Thinking out-loud, "Is it worth it?" She would spend the day working on displays and ordering new yarns for the upcoming holiday rush.

Knitters and the like have a "personal time clock" gene, and they usually go nuts with "family Christmas orders" by October. They place all of this holiday stress on themselves, of course, as their families would be just as happy with anything small, or even just to see their Grandma happy, relaxed, and enjoying the moments rather than working themselves to death.

Like all retail, most of The Yarn Shop sales were received in the last quarter of the year. Weather had a lot to do with it too; not just the holidays. Nobody sane knitted a warm afghan in August: one waited until November when you could keep warm with the darn thing on your lap and gently draping it across your knees while you knitted away.

It was an important time to make sure everything was in order at The Yarn shop.

"Gotta put our best foot forward this holiday season," Judy announced to no one and shuddering at the thought of another sales drop this month. She plopped down her ipad and tote bag of notes and a few coffee supplies on the floor next to the table and sat down in her chair.

What to do first, she thought, as she inspected the family of rats in front of her. One by one, she looked at them: they were all there but something was different. She leaned forward and looked more closely.

She regarded them closely: "That's not how I left them." They had been rearranged!

The rats were all in different positions, and they were all staring straight ahead; not like she had left them: all facing each other as if in deep conversation. "Huh."

Judy thought about the activity in the shop since the last Rat Day Tuesday. Only knitters, crocheters, some weavers, and a few fiber arts members had visited, and none of them were into rats. So why and who would arrange them all differently? Maybe they were just having fun, she thought. It's easy to do. The rats are so inviting, and like Geraldine did, you want to pick them up with both hands cupping them for a closer inspection and move them around. They were fun to play with.

Then she looked at LeBeau. Where was his licorice candy? Surely, someone didn't EAT it! It had to have been sitting out on the table maybe three days! Judy shook her head and dismissed the whole thing, thinking, "It takes all kinds, I guess!" She put away the coffee supplies, then pulled out her yarn inventory sheets and switched the ipad to 'calculator' and went to work.

The day went by quickly and she got a lot done. Not having but a couple of customers with special requests and questions to interrupt her, Judy whizzed through her day's to-do list and even had time to send her daughter in Dallas an email telling her about the rats. "I wonder what she will think about the Makers and their great rat adventure?" she thought.

Judy made the call, but like always, she had to leave a message. Her daughter was involved in the fast lane with the kids, just like all the other young Moms today. They didn't have much time for anything except the challenge of being a good parent.

"Hi there. Just touching base. Call me when you got a few minutes; I've got a story to tell ya."

She tucked away the ipad and sat at her own gathering table. Judy pulled out some magazines from the shelf and concentrated on photos of a few Thanksgiving display ideas. Her creative genes took over.

She stood up and walked around the loft looking at her work: The shelves were reorganized, the spinning wheels and swifts were relocated for a newer look. Now she had a great idea to decorate the table for Thanksgiving, and it wouldn't cost her a thing! The rats would be the center piece!
She pulled out her box of decor from her back room and rummaged through, locating some leaves and gourds left over from a craft session last year. Judy smiled and repeated to herself out-loud, her favorite saying born from

these challenging economic times: "What I have is What I need!"

Using one of her own finished sample lace shawls with fall color, she spread it across the table, showing the fan and feather pattern (maybe she will even sell some shawl kits with fall yarn colors!) and then placed the leaves and gourds in the middle.

Now for the rats. "THIS time, I will make sure I know where every rat is sitting, and who is talking to whom," she thought.

Oh, Judy is a good marketer. You have to be, these days. Owners of small stores like The Yarn Shop work very, very hard. Your business had better be your passion. Providing quality merchandise not found at the big-box stores, special services such as the classes she and DD taught, and simply just being there seven days a week to help customers is sometimes not enough, and only the best survive.

Judy is one of the best and her customers come from sometimes fifty miles away. Not only will she sell some shawl kits, she may be able to get another rat class going too! "Great idea, kiddo!" she praised herself.

She picked up her own three rats, Chloe, Lenny and Violet in her arms and one at a time and placed them in position on the gourds. Next was DD's Ratcliff and her new little Belle and Raspberry's Rattina. Then, she grabbed LeBeau and the Sheriff, placing them next to the little girls. Let's see...where will I put Pierre, Echo, El Ratoncito Perez (why did Sandy name him this, anyway)! And Anita's little no-name wonder?

She looked at the group. The rats were spaced too far apart; not good for a center display, and her customers needed more work space on the table in front of each chair. She needed to regroup.

Starting over, Judy thought about the scene she was creating. The rats need to be doing something. But what? Then it hit her: They needed to be having a conversation like the makers do when they are sitting at the table!

Someone needs to be giving direction, and the rest of the rats are listening intently, just like she does with her rat instruction! She picked up Pierre and pointed a finger at him. "You will be the teacher!" She said out loud and placed him on the highest gourd in a nest of orange and rust yarn.

Then, as if they were all in a classroom, she arranged the rats below Pierre at his feet, and made sure they were all watching Pierre with eyes centered and listening to every word he had to say. Perfect! These are his students! They all fit in nice and tight, and the fan and flame shawl shows off nicely, too.

Sitting back in her director's chair, Judy admired her work. She looked at her creation, then thought about LeBeau and his missing licorice. "Hmmmm." Marna will be looking for that.

Getting up, Judy went to the coffee shelf behind the curtain in the back of the room. It was still there. She picked up the little bag of Dutch candies Marna had left her, opened the bag and pulled out one of the little sour black morsels and replaced the lost licorice with a new one. Now, everything was perfect.

61

So she could show her husband Ned when she got home and send an email photo to her daughter, Judy pulled out her iphone and leaned over the table for a family group shot of the rats. Click, click .

"Take a couple of extras, just to be sure," she thought. She tried a couple of angles. Click, click click. "Who knows? Maybe I can use the photos in a brochure someday."

The shelves were tidy and neat. The new orders for holiday yarns and supplies were placed. Judy's Thanksgiving table display was a masterpiece. Her shop looked just great. She sighed, content with her work for the day. Hopefully her efforts would generate some good sales. The court house tower clock struck five. It was time to wrap it up and head home. Maybe she could even catch the end of the Cowboy's game with Ned.

Judy packed up, and headed for the door. As Geraldine would say, "Avoir, mes amis! A bientot!"
"Goodbye, my friends!" Until later!

Chapter Eight

Lessons in the Yarn Shop

The rain let up around ten o'clock, but a heavy cloud cover guaranteed nobody would be enjoying the famous Texas starlight and heavens above. It was a dark and dreary night.

The Grandville Square and all the stores stood quietly behind their slick cobbled sidewalks. Inside The Yarn Shop, the loft was also very dark. So dark, in fact, that if you wanted to move around, you had to feel your way and creep around slowly, reaching out for the walls and familiar fixtures until you found the light switch.

The only illumination came from outside on the street, and that was only the dim light from the antique street pole perched just outside The Art Gallery front door. The beam reached inside The Yarn Shop and touched the stairway.

No sounds in the shop were heard except the clock ticking in the corner. Tic, tic, tic... You could hear the second hand swing to the number six and then it made a clacking sound, missed a beat, then moved again to the seven twice as fast to catch up to stay on time.

Outside, The Square was empty of cars. No sounds here either; just the traffic signal switching silently from red to green to amber over and over again, without any cars ever going through the intersection.

The great courthouse flags; one Texas and one United States hung limp against the pole and tangled with each other.

There was no wind of any kind to be heard. No movement. Just an eerie suffocating stillness.

The courthouse tower clock and inside, The Yarn Shop's corner clock struck midnight simultaneously. The tower clock sang out loud, disturbing some pigeons on the roof and the Yarn Shop's clock simply rang the hour. Twelve bells. These were the only sounds.

The light in the yarn shop suddenly switched on. Pierre sat high on his gourd and slowly turned his head from side to side, and then he blinked his eyes. All by himself.

He seemed to be exercising his neck, as if he were stiff with arthritis or something. Next, he lifted his right arm, and looked at his hand, then his left; repeated this action until they seemed to work to his satisfaction. He rubbed his sore neck. He wiggled his feet. Stretched his legs. Then, comfortable with his new ability to move, looked down upon all of his little fur comrades.

He gently hopped off his gourd, leaned forward and then he whispered ever so quietly, "Bonjour, mes amis!"

None of the other rats moved. At first. Then, after what seemed a long time to Pierre, LeBeau turned his head too, just like Pierre, and went through the very same actions. LeBeau looked at the table in front of him and spied the licorice candy. "What's this?" were his first words.

Pierre studied LeBeau for a moment and turned to look at the candy, then, "Votre bon bon!"

LeBeau picked up the candy, and looking straight up at Pierre, distrusting, squinted his eyes. Then turning to the side, he tucked it under his arm secretly to hide it; perhaps to take it somewhere else. Then he scrambled farther away from Pierre.

Just then, ALL the rats began to turn their heads and stretch, as if they were all waking up from a sound sleep. They repeated the very same actions as Pierre and LeBeau. Now they seem to be hopping all around the table with greetings and hugs.

Anyone could see: They were saying hello and getting acquainted. Did they already know each other? Or were they meeting for the first time?

"L'attention! L'attention!" shouted Pierre. Everyone looked at Pierre.

Sheriff TEX questioned, "Whaaaattttt????"

Chloe turned and whispered, "I think he means, 'attention,' everyone."

Everyone stopped talking and looked at Pierre. Together, "So......?"

Pierre bowed and in his most polite voice, "Bon soir. Je m'appelle Pierre. Je suis le proffesseur"! No one answered; they just looked at each other in question.

Then El Ratoncito Perez, who hailed from Spain, thought he knew what Pierre was saying, as French and Spanish are similar.

"I think his name is Pierre, and he wants to be our teacher, you know, like, the professor," he said.

"Whale, A'll be da-gone!" responded Sheriff TEX from the back of the group. Sheriff Tex grinned with his big ear-to ear full tooth smile. He put his hands on his hips. "If y'all are the teecher, than how you gonna teech when all ya speak is Frennnnnch? Huh...?"

Pierre reached up and smoothed his mustache, blinked his eyes, adjusted his black beret, and leaned in to his little miniature classroom of students. With complete confidence, he ever so gently informed, "J'apprend le Francais de raet!" Everybody just sat there starring.

"Whaaaattttt????" questioned the Sheriff.

Again, Pierre said very slowly, just one word at a time, "J apprend ..."

El Ratoncito interrupted, "I think that means teach!" he shouted.

You would think they were playing a great game of charades. Everyone wanted to guess what Pierre ways saying.

Pierre continued, "Le Francais raet."

Again, El Ratoncito, "That means French, so raet must mean rat!"

From the back of the group, Echo shouted, HE WILL TEACH US RAT FRENCH!!!" Echo won the Charades game.

Pierre jumped up and down, clapping his hands and nodding his head. "Oui! Oui! Naturalement!" "But of Course!"

Everyone was so excited, and now they were all talking at once.

"How is he going to do this?" Asked Chloe.

Raspberry agreed. She wasn't so sure she even WANTED to learn Rat French. "I don't know..."

El Ratoncito Perez was comforting. "It's not that hard," he said. "Besides, Pierre sounds like he has only simple easy words for us to learn; like his French is limited, or something...."

Chloe agreed. "Yes, I mean, oui. I think you are right. Like he only says 'hello,' and what his name is, and things like that. Like he's a 'first year French' student."

Echo, climbing down from her gourd, just wanted everyone to be open with the idea. She did not like any discord. "You know, we love our new life here in The Yarn Shop, and we have all the time in the world; it will be fun to try this French thing out."

Sheriff TEX rounded everyone up. "All raght, then. Y'all can vote. Those that want Rat Frennnch , raise yer hand." All the rats lifted their front right hands. Even Sheriff TEX raised his own hand. It was unanimous. Rat French would be the night language in The Yarn Shop.

That being settled, LeBeau quickly hopped down from his display gourd, grabbed hold of a support beam next to the table, and like a fireman sliding down his pole, quickly shimmied down the distance to the slippery wood floor below.

He scurried to a wall shelf and carefully scanned the stacks of yarn in the lower cubicle, spied his target and leaped into a pile of soft yellow and orange mohair blend. LeBeau nosed his way deep into the yarn and completely disappeared into the ball of yellow fluff. Only the end of his tail stuck out and it wiggled back and forth as he worked.

Nobody saw him, as he secretly eased the licorice candy from under his arm and with both hands, gently placed it safely in a little nest adding it to the other piece he stashed here the last time. "Ahhhh," he thought. "Now I have two bon bons!"

Up on the table, a loud buzz of rat French was underway. You could hear Pierre above the others, "But of Course! Naturalement! Tres bien!"

As the rat group talked excitedly about their new rat French lessons, LeBeau popped his head out of the yellow mohair, tiptoed across the floor to the support beam and promptly found it too high and slippery to scale vertically. Oh, no!

Last time, there was a basket of yarn balls on the floor that provided "steps" up the support beam and back to the table. But not this time. Somebody moved the yarn basket and with no one noticing his absence, LeBeau was forced to stay right where he was: under the table.

It was getting early. The rats knew they only had until six o'clock to make it back to their places on the table, and it was already five.

Pierre was finishing up his first rat French lesson. "Je prend ma place," he said. Pierre demonstrated taking his seat on his gourd. He hopped off, then back on, saying while hopping, "Je prend ma place!" "I take my seat." The class repeated after Pierre, and then found their way back to their display gourd on the table.

"Je regard autour de moi" (I look all around me) this time, the rats repeated what Pierre said, but they were unsure of the meaning, until Pierre showed them to look all around themselves; then they knew. They all looked around themselves. "Je regard autour de moi."

That's when they noticed LeBeau was gone.

"Ou est LeBeau?" asked Pierre.

This was easy. "Where is LeBeau?" They loudly said in unison.

"Le Beau! WHERE IS LE BEAU?"

Way below them, at the foot of the support beam, was their comrade.

"HELP! HELP"!

The rats jumped from their display gourds and ran to the table's edge, and there he was, sitting on his back legs with his arms outstretched up to them.

Pierre shouted, "Aidez il!" and LeBeau responded, "yes, Help me! Sil vous plait! PLEASE!"

Somehow, El Ratoncito Perez knew exactly what to do. (How come?) He was an expert in nighttime activity and seemed quite the acrobat, but no one knew why.

"Roll one of those balls of heavy stock yarn over here!" he commanded.

Four rats rolled and pushed an attractive super-bulky weight variegated fall color yarn (it looked like hemp) over to El Ratoncito, who then pulled the end out of the middle of the skein with his teeth and ran with it to the center table display.

He tied it tightly to a heavy part of the display, then ran back to the yarn ball. Then, he pushed the skein over the table and it landed right at LeBeau's feet. Whoa. Talk about precision. He was really good at this!

Rantoncito looked down at Le Beau.

"Push the yarn ball around the table leg a couple of times, and make a knot."

LeBeau followed instruction, then surprisingly, he knew the perfect knot to use: A sailor's bowline would pull the yarn very tight, and would secure the ball to the table leg. "Its like throwing a line over a pylon!" LeBeau said with confidence. "The more you pulled, the tighter the knot would become."

Back up on the table, the rest of the rats jumped on the yarn ball and pushed it around the center display for weight. What a team.

Ratoncito gave the "go ahead" signal.

LeBeau made his climb back to join his comrades.

Whale a'll be dammed"! Shouted the Sheriff.

They were all back up on the table again, but they wondered about LeBeau's private little adventure.

"What were y'all doin down thare?" asked Sheriff TEX.

"Pas maintenant!" Interrupted Pierre. Not Now! Everyone agreed. Time was of the essence. They could talk later; they needed to get the yarn ball back and put everything back where it belonged on the table. It was already five-forty-five.

Together, they tugged and tugged on the yarn line and El Ratoncito's sailor's bowline held strong.

"I told you"......he said.

Together, they made an unanimous rat decision: Using their incisors as scissors, Sheriff TEX and Echo with their heads together and with cheeks touching, easily snipped the yarn thread from the skein, and it fell to the floor. And that's where it would stay, for now, anyway.

They HAD to get back to "their places" right now. They pushed the skein back in place, and sped back to their own display gourd positions without a second to spare. Talk about timing.

The corner clock struck six o'clock. The second hand swung to the number six; made a clacking sound, missed a beat, then moved again to the seven twice as fast to catch up to stay on time.

And then, all was still. The light automatically went out. No sounds, no movement. The rats were back in the Thanksgiving display and on their gourd positions; each one looking dead straight ahead. Motionless. All was quiet again in The Yarn Shop.

Chapter Nine

Fashion Show

DD Bench usually worked Mondays. This gave her partner Judy some rest, and she really earned it this week. The Thanksgiving display was outstanding!

The gourds and leaves were the perfect display props to back up the array of vibrant new fall yarns that had just come in. And the rats!

"You all look so cute" she said aloud. How darling they did Look, like they were having a dinner party right there in the middle of the table! She thought, with this display, she'd surely be taking large holiday yarn orders by the end of the day!

She planned to take it a little slower today. For some reason, DD just hurt all over. She grabbed a chair and sat down. "Aleve. Where's my Aleve?"

She had two shots of cortisone injected into each knee last Friday and it was finally beginning to work. "Maybe I'll order my lunch in today," she thought. "I'll spend time at the table getting orders all straight for the busy season ahead."

She looked at the rat collection closely, and shook her head back and forth. "Who would have thought?" she asked out loud. That's when she noticed the strand of yarn on the floor.

DD bent over to pick up the yarn, but found it tied tight to the table leg. "Hmmmmm. Judy must have had a "Yarn fart!" Most knitters know, a yarn fart is a major snarl in a skein of yarn, and when discovered, is always announced with a very loud "Oh shit!" It's a mess; usually takes hours to untangle. Sometimes you have to tie one end of the skein to a chair or table leg, tug it tight and slowly pick at the snarling mess from across the room until you can finally find the other end and get it untangled (Caution: You NEVER want to do this while drinking wine). Poor Judy: she must have had a real time with this one. She grabbed her scissors and cut the yarn free, tossing it into the trash.

The day was surprisingly busy. She made lots of sales for fall and Christmas; but the REAL shocker was all of the customers who wanted to sign up for the NEXT RAT CLASS!

The rats were the real stars of the day. Judy's centerpiece was the best marketing tool ever invented! Brilliant! By the end of the day, six more ladies had signed up to make a rat, and they were all waiting to hear when they would schedule another rat class. They had left talking about fur and eyes and even what they would name their rat! It was unbelievable.

This rat business was just too good! She had to figure out a way to persuade the makers to leave all their rats here on the table. The rats were the best sales magnet, ever! Ratmaking must be some kind of contagious disease!

She checked her watch. DD always closed the shop promptly at five on Mondays as she had a teddy bear class to teach at the art center in town. If she left now, she would have just enough time to pick up a brown bag taco dinner at Fred's and feed her dogs before Teddy Bear time.

On the way out, she waived "bye" to Samantha who was busy on the phone with a customer. She nodded silently and waived back without missing a word on the phone. The chime on the door bell sang softly and DD was gone for the day.

Tuesday arrived too fast for Judy. Still worn out from decorating the shop and overseeing a fiber show in Dallas over the weekend, she toted extra supplies up the stairway for the rat session that afternoon.

Even though it was early she was already hungry. Lousy diet. Who can live on grapefruit juice and a crunchy piece of stale wheat bread? Hopefully some of the Makers will bring some fresh baked banana bread or something. Muffins or cookies. At least something sweet!

The Makers were to put the last touches on their rats and bring the clothes and accessories they all had made at home. "This should be SOME fashion show," she said with a musical tone to herself.

If there had been any activity in the shop last night, Judy did not notice. Her display appeared just as she left it, untouched, with the exception of DD's note, sitting on the table by the display, and the fact that Marna's candy was missing again. Out loud, "Now I know who likes that black candy!" she said.

She picked up the note:

What a day! We nearly sold out of the fall color yarns and the rest of the fish-hat kits, along with all the

75

needles that go with them! Look at the order book. But the REAL news is the interest in the RATS! Six more ladies signed up for your NEXT RAT CLASS! You better get one on the calendar fast. This display is magical! Everyone just gravitated to it, and if thy didn't buy yarn or order some, they signed up to make a rat! You're a genius! Love, DD.

Judy laughed, picked up the note and held it to her chest with a big smile, bending down and looking at the fur collection. "You little guys certainly ARE magical!" Then she forgot about being hungry and began to get the table and the supplies ready for her class of rat makers.

Raspberry arrived first, carrying her tote of knitting supplies and she had Rattina's new accessories to show and tell. The Makers all agreed they would wait till they all arrived and share these together. As she took a spot at the table, the rest came through the art gallery doors all in a burst together. They must have met in the Square's parking lot at the same time and nearly caused a traffic commotion coming across the street.

Geraldine came through the doors in a storm, swinging her arms like she was far away, and nobody could see or hear her. But there she was, just two feet away, shouting. *"Bonjour mes amis!* Comment allez-vous? Je suis magnifique!"

Sandy moved back two steps. "Oh my God, now it starts...."

Geraldine swung her tote bag teasingly along her side, "Guess what I have...?" and followed the ladies up the stairway. (Like she was the only one with a rat!)

"Someday we will all chip in and buy an elevator", Katy groaned.

They collected themselves at the gathering table, starring, open mouthed. "Wow!" Marna picked up her little LeBeau. "Dey all look so good here in dis Tanksgiving display!" She noticed his candy was missing again.

Raspberry was admiring for everyone. "Judy, this is just adorable," she said. "They look like they are all having Thanksgiving dinner together! We love it!"

Marna sat down in her spot. "Looks like someone already else had dessert! LeBeau's candy is gone, again."

"Oh, I know now who likes your candy, Marna. It's DD. She worked yesterday and must have eaten it as a snack." Marna nodded. "Yes, eeder dat or a hungry customer with good taste!"

They all laughed, and settled down in their seats; each eager to show and tell their rat fashions.

So much for LeBeau's licorice candy.

Like the great teacher she was, Judy asked her class, "Okay, who wants to go first?"

Raspberry announced she was first to arrive and ready. She immediately pulled out of her tote, Rattina's little artist palette, tiny brushes, and a smock she had sewn. "We now have a resident rat artist in The Yarn Shop!" She put Rattina's smock on, moved her arms to hold the palette and brushes; then returned her back to her place in the display. Everyone applauded. "Bravo!"

77

Rattina looked just like a miniature Raspberry!

Sandy wanted to go next. "Remember the Today Show story about El Ratoncito Perez in Spain? He's the mouse that is the equivalent our Tooth Fairy?

That's the little guy I named my rat for: El Ratoncito Perez, and I have made him a little necklace to carry his collected babies teeth and pearls."

"Aren't you going to make him any clothes?" Raspberry asked.

"Ratoncito has to move very quickly at night, so clothes would be too cumbersome. He is very secretive you know, and he works alone; no partners for him. He's like a sleuth! I may make him a mask later, in case anyone might recognize him during the day, and perhaps a knapsack for his pearls."

Katy picked up Echo and tied a little green apron on her. She added a straw hat with a tiny dandelion flower sticking out from the brim. She was the perfect little garden rat. Very environmental; ready to save the world, or plant something beautiful; one or the other. Katy edged Echo over to LeBeau's side. "What do you think, Lebeau?"

"You are soooooo--oo pretty!" Marna made LeBeau spin around, then put a very smart hat and jacket on him; Dutch-style, of course, with a pocket just big enough for a licorice candy.

Geraldine was so excited; she was sitting far forward on the edge her chair, vibrating with anxiousness and about to fall off. She just couldn't stand it. Even though she was at the back of the table, she just had to go next.

She pulled a tiny black felt beret from her Louis Vuitton bag, along with a miniature black knitted wool scarf and held them ready in her hand. Geraldine was chomping at the bit. She stood up, rudely reached out over Marna , and grabbed Pierre from his gourd.

First, she tied on the scarf. And then, for her piece de resistance, added the beret. *"Parfaitement!"* she shouted. Oh, perfect. If this wasn't enough, next she pulled out a tiny bit of black fuzz, twisted it into shape, and held it to Pierre's face. "This will be his mustache!" she said. Before the day was over she would sew it on Pierre, just below his nose. But of course.

Next, Sheriff TEX donned a little leather vest with a tiny Texas star, along with a miniature Stetson hat. Mary Ellen had searched all over Fort Worth looking for that darn hat, and finally found it, wouldn't cha know, right there in Grandville at the Cowboy Markethouse shop right next door on the Square. And his little leather-like boots were discovered in her Granddaughter's box of Barbie clothes. She held her rat up for all to see: "Okay, Y'all! I'm in charge here, and y'all better not forget that!"

All eyes were on Anita. Who was her rat, anyway? They all waited for her whole story.

Anita grinned with a wise smile. "Okay, I've got it!" She walked over to the middle of the group and reached between Mary Ellen and Sandy, picking up her little fuzzy friend.

"Let me introduce little Miss Amelia EarRat! She is quite the little career rat and like me, she flies airplanes all over the world for a living. I found this Barbie-doll jacket and hat that looks a lot like mine! How lucky is that?"

79

Everybody was laughing now, and applauding Anita.

Judy jumped up. Her eyes were wide and she held her hands up as if to stop all the action in a play, "Just a minute! Don't anybody move! I'll be right back!" She bounded down the stairs as fast as she could holding the rail with both hands, just to be safe, along the way.

Everyone just looked at each other. "What?"

She returned moments later with a silver antique toy airplane from the gift area in the gallery. It looked just like the one that Amelia Earhart had flown: it was a replica of a Lockheed Model 10 Electra.

"I think Amelia would look perfect sitting in this!" Judy said with pride.

"Unbelievable!"

Anita proudly stood up and placed Amelia in her little plane. She fit perfectly.
"All she needs is a scarf and a set of goggles!"

Cheers and lots of clapping, Everyone agreed. Anita's little fly girl looked right at home.

With the exception of DD's first rat Belle, who would be back next week, all the rats were now properly outfitted, and the makers leaned back and admired their handiwork. Talk about talent. The rat fashion show was over, and the ladies placed their little fur friends back in the display. Time for coffee and cake. Some had wine and cheese but all had a ball and the season had definitely begun.

As if by magic, "Why don't we leave them here for the holidays?" asked Kate, who just refilled her wine glass. "They all look like they just belong."

The Makers passed the cups and cake around. Not many takers for the coffee; they really enjoyed their wine.

There was no reason to disagree. The rats were at home, that's for sure. Besides, it was time to get back to knitting and finishing up all of their Christmas presents. What with the weeks it took to make a rat, all the Makers were way behind on their gift lists.

They were very happy. Their rats were finished; they had their cake and coffee, and were ready to wrap it up.

All packed up for the day, they followed Judy down the stairs, chuckling and congratulating each other on their fabulous rat work. What a day!

"Au Revoir mes amis! A Bientot!" they all said. My god, now they WERE ALL speaking Geraldine's French!

Chapter Ten

Sir Reginald

Tic, tic tic..... The second hand darted to the number six, made a clacking sound, missed a beat, then moved again to the seven twice as fast to catch up to stay on time. The clock in the corner struck twelve. The Tower Clock in the Square sang out. The light in the Yarn Shop switched on.

The rats took turns slowing waking up. The process was always the same: They opened their eyes; they slowly turned their heads from side to side, stretched their hands and legs and wiggled their feet. They appeared to check themselves for complete working capability and then hopped off their gourds and scurried from their places in the Thanksgiving display to an open space on the table top.

Today, they all gathered in a circle and checked each other's new additions: Pierre now had a mustache, not to mention a beret and a scarf!

"OOOOhhhh, you are tres handsome, Pierre!" sighed Chloe, and ran to his side.

Pierre straightened up very tall, leaning sideways to closely inspect her backside. "Naturellement, mon Cherie...." He noticed her French had improved. "Tres bon amelioration!" Nice improvement. He held her hand up and kissed it.

Sheriff TEX strutted his stuff for all to see. He took several steps forward, stopped, turned around several times, and held his arms out to his sides. "Ah giss thare's no question whose in charge here, raght - er...N'est pas"?

Again, Pierre noticed the improved French, even from Sheriff TEX.

Rattina twirled. She loved her smock and pallet of colors, and held a brush in her hand. Ratcliff, Violet and Chloe, who already had attire from the beginning, joined her. "Are you going to paint us?" They posed together, thinking they were the perfect subjects.

Echo loved her apron and hat, but thought they might be a little too "showy." Not one to make a big scene, she was nervous, and took a couple of steps back inside the group.

"I do hope my maker got these from the Goodwill store, or at least they were hand-me-downs from some little girl's doll." Later, she found out, they WERE from a classic children's book and character, 'Linnea's Garden.' Echo looked a little like Linnea!

But, Amelia, was the real star of the group with her antique Electra airplane. The three "Ratskateers," AKA El Ratoncito Perez, LeBeau, and Lenny gathered around her and rubbed the side of the plane lovingly. "Might-tee-fine, might-tee-fine!" LeBeau was doubtful. "Does it fly?"

Amelia hopped off. "Of course, it does, when I AM READY TO FLY HER!" she said, rather matter of fact. She strutted by the Ratskateers and joined all the girl rats.
The rats paraded around in a circle, showing off to each other singing "Easter Parade."

Suddenly they heard another voice from below in the gallery. They all froze, bumping into each other into a clump. Pierre was knocked down by LeBeau and nearly fell off the edge of the table.

"Sacre Bleu!" he shouted, looking up at LeBeau. "Excusez-moi" apologized Pierre, picking himself up. He knew he just swore, but LeBeau didn't know that word yet, thank goodness. They all listened intently.

Sheriff TEX put his hand to his mouth.

"Y'all....Shhhhhhhh!"

"Hey, what about me? What about me?" They all heard... someone....

Sheriff TEX squinted his eyes, searching all around the table. Nothing. He instructed all the rats to hush. "Whaaat about Whooooo?" he asked cautiously.

"Me! Look down here! My name's Sir Reginald and I live below! Look! Down here in the gallery! What about me? I have clothes and I want to show you mine, too! Can you come see me? Jump off the table! Come and look over the edge of the loft. Look! I'm right here!"

The rats all looked at each other in amazement and made an immediate rat decision. Who was this Sir Reginald rat guy? Where did he come from? How come he was down there, and they were up here? They needed to find out. Immediately.

Using the basket (now mysteriously back in place at the bottom of the table) of soft skeins of yarn as a mattress, they leaped from the table and tumbled into the yarn basket below. Some of the yarn balls fell out with their arrivals but they didn't care. They were all off the table and on the wooden floor of the Yarn Shop.

"Over here! Over here!" Sir Reginald shouted. They rushed to the loft railing.

"Ohhh, this looks scary" questioned Echo. She hesitated, not ready to move any farther.

They looked down, and there he was. A pert little brown rat who looked just like them, only he had a little waist coat and wore a pair of spectacles. He must have been English. Very Londonderry. Very proper, indeed.

Sir Reginald! Of course. Samantha's gift rat from Judy. He was standing right below them looking up at the group. "Can you come down?" he asked.

"All of Us?" they returned in mass shock response. "I'td be better if y'all came up," responded the sheriff. "Yer just one, and we are a whole group up here," he confirmed. "We could throw ya a rope, and you could come up fer a visit"

The rats agreed. A lot safer this way. Much easier for him to come to them; besides, they had to figure out how they would all get back up on the table as it was.

Sheriff TEX looked around, searching for just the right rope-re, yarn. LeBeau and El Ratoncito were already practiced in these skills, so they knew just which yarn to use. They grabbed the familiar hemp-like skein and rolled it over to the loft's edge.

The boys then wound the ball around the railing a few times, anchoring it in the now-famous "LeBeau Bowline secure knot," and then tossed the yarn tail down to Sir Reginald, who grabbed it quickly and secured it to a table leg on the gallery floor.

The trip was a piece of cake for him. Sir Reginald used his arms up and over, up and over, making the climb to the top in no time at all. "Whew! Jolly good!" he said, falling right in front of Rattina, Chloe, and Amelia.

"Well, aren't you a cutie!" said Rattina, always the flirt, with her hands on her hips.

Sir Reginald was shy, as these were the first rats he had ever met. His spectacles fell to the floor, and he bent over and picked them up. He Bowed, with one hand in front and one hand in back; most politely.

"Sir Reginald, at your service, Mum!" He WAS English!

"What do you DO down there?" They all wanted to know.

He sat on a skein of soft baby alpaca and started his story. "First, I protect the books," he said. "And, I make sure the printer works all the time and most importantly, I keep the sales records straight for Samantha," he said.

"You might say I'm kind of like her Secret Good Luck Charm, but she doesn't know it," he concluded. "Samantha keeps me at her desk, or perched her printer. Sometimes when the printer has a problem, subconsciously she picks me up from the desk, and puts me on the printer, and then, you know, it works just fine! She's very superstitions, you know".

"Whale, A'll be da-gone!" Sheriff TEX was amazed.

And so was everybody else. So there WAS another rat downstairs. "And an English one, at that! And smart, ta boot! "

"Too bad you have to live all by yourself down there," said Echo. Always the care giver, she wanted to know, "Could you come up here and live with us in the Yarn Shop?"

"Oh no, my place is in the gallery, keeping everything straight for Samantha. She really has no idea just how much work I REALLY do for her. It would be a mess! And now, I need to get back to my place on the printer." He made his way over to the yarn rope.

They all followed and huddled around him as he grabbed the rope. Reluctantly, they bid their goodbyes. Sir Reginald headed downward while Violet and Bella stood watching and holding hands.

"Wait!" shouted El Ratoncito. "We need to fix the rope so you can come up easy next time." He took the ball of yarn and rolled it over scooting it into the bottom shelf of the yarn bin where it could not be seen. Next, he slid the rope over to the corner of the loft rail and secured it behind a spinner wheel. You would never know it was there. "When you get to the bottom, take the rope over to the side and hide it out of view so no one knows its down there," he said.

Sir Reginald did as he was told. When he reached the bottom, he swung the rope over to the side and hid it behind a display of art glass antiques and some children's fashions. Completely out of view. "Mission completed!" He yelled at his highest voice upstairs to the group. Then he slipped into the back room and hopped on the printer.

He had to check for errors in the sales report tonight, and make corrections before Samantha returned in the morning. "What a job," he thought, "but someone's got to do it! Heavens! The whole place would fall apart without me!"

Above in the loft, fourteen little rats lined up along the ledge like a bunch of scarecrows on a telephone line.

As soon as Sir Reginald was out of sight, and they were satisfied he made it back to the printer safely, they would now make their way back up to the table top and the Thanksgiving display.

But how to do this? They all looked at each other with wonder. El Ratoncito jumped up. "No problem-0!" What an acrobat. Kind of a show-off, too. With his arms held high, and his legs wound tightly just so, he demonstrated how easy it was to scale the table pole from the yarn basket on the floor.

"First you jump in the basket, then climb over these yarn balls here, then grab the table leg here, and put your hands over your hands, pulling yourself up. Before you know it, you're here!" He was already on the table top waving his crew on. "See? Easy! Hurry on up! "

One by one and ladies first, they all followed Ratoncito's instruction and before they knew it, they were all back on the table and lined up for Pierre's daily French lesson. Today, they would learn to count. "Un, deux, trios, quatre, cinq" started Pierre.

And so it went. One, two, three, four five. Together, they all learned to count in Rat French. "Six, sept, huit, neuf, dix....." Six, seven, eight, nine, ten.

Tic, tic tic..... The second hand swung to the number six, made a clacking sound, missed a beat, then moved again to the seven twice as fast to catch up to stay on time. The big tower clock in the Square chimed in simultaneously. Six o'clock, and time to go to sleep.

Chapter Eleven

Season's Greetings

Thanksgiving was just around the corner. The knitters were consumed with family gatherings and their days at The Yarn Shop were fewer.

Judy looked at DD. "Well, where is everybody?"

"It's always like this, the week before Thanksgiving, Judy. You know that. The knitters are busy planning their own family dinners and making the drive to who knows where to see the grandkids."

"Then this is the perfect day to decorate the shop's tree! What do you want the theme to be this year?"

They were standing in the art gallery below trying hard to come up with an idea. Samantha surprised them. "Why don't you do your tree down here with me and decorate it with the rats?"

DD and Judy turned and looked at each other. "You know, Judy's Thanksgiving table display with the rats has brought us more business than selling yarn this month!"

Samantha nodded her head affirmatively. "My suggestion, exactly. Go get the rats, and let's put them in my tree, which is already set up. We don't have to have two trees and you don't have to do a thing!"

Judy went up to get the rats. DD's knees were hurting again. She had to get a big basket, as there were now so many. She picked up Chloe first, "Her first baby" she said, and then gathered the rest in her arms, placing them in the basket.

In no time, she was headed back down the stairway, holding carefully to the rickety railing. This was a good habit. One false step and life as she knew it would be gone forever. She hated the steps more each day, and wondered if they were a factor in the shrinking business. The customers surely complained about them all the time.

Samantha took the basket from Judy's arms. "You know, people are coming in and asking about your rat class. When are you going to do this again?" She looked at Judy.

"We've got to get through the holidays, and then in January we will schedule another rat group. Everyone has had so much fun with these, and they are all so different, even though they were made from the same pattern."

Judy picked up Pierre. "This one is Geraldine's. Can you believe it? This rat only speaks French!"

All three ladies gave a hoot. "What a riot!" DD picked up Sheriff TEX and held him up to Samantha. "Look at this guy: Guess who made him?"

Samantha did not know the rat makers well. "I couldn't guess, but, most likely one of the gals that comes in each week from Fort Worth, right?"

"You got it: Mary Ellen Afton. With all the European rats, we mentioned we needed a real Texas rat, and she came through.

She say's her rat doesn't mess around and that he really runs the show." They all laughed as DD reached up and put

Sheriff TEX in a nice spot in the tree next to a velvet and pearl trimmed pillow.

The rest of the rats soon found places in the Art Gallery Christmas tree, along with many other gift-giving treasures for customers to ogle over.

Judy put a chef's hat on LeBeau, and gave him a little wooden spoon to hold. He looked like he was looking for the kitchen.

DD looked up at Judy. "We need Amelia's airplane, and a few balls of holiday yarns with silver and gold trims." Back upstairs Judy climbed.

Huffing now, "Anything else while I am up here?" She hollered from the loft.

"Let's put a spinning wheel at the base of the tree. And how about some of those drop spindles? What a great gift idea for a knitter!"

The ladies worked together and the tree was finished in no time at all. A combined effort of The Art Gallery and The Yarn Shop above, the "co-op tree" was a masterpiece. The rats looked at home and happy with all the other decor and gift ideas.

Samantha went behind the tree and turned the lights on. It was magical! Twinkle, twinkle, and just enough light to highlight everything in the tree without it becoming a beacon in the middle of the store. They were very pleased with themselves. "We are great!"

"Tree decorating makes me hungry! Let's go for Tacos," suggested DD.

"Good idea!" Judy grabbed her purse, leaving Samantha to admire her tree and mind the gallery. They headed down their cobbled street to the local Taco Spot in town for a quick to-go lunch.

Samantha was happy to work with her knitter friends. She knew they didn't really have any space in the loft to add a Christmas tree as their customers bumped into things around that gathering table as it was.

Besides, having the tree downstairs kept people in her store longer, and they would surely find something they couldn't resist.

"You've got to keep them in the store as long as you can," She reminded herself, and headed to the cash wrap desk as the door swung open and a customer walked in.

The door swung opened and a rush of crisp winter air came in. "I came to see the rats," she said with a demanding monotone, looking around the shop.

"Oh! We just put them in the Christmas tree! They are our ornaments!" explained Samantha with a warm smile guiding her to the lighted tree.

The woman walked quickly behind Samantha, secretly reaching for something in her leather tote. She struggled for a moment, pulling out a small digital camera and checking the settings. Samantha turned around and looked at her, surprised.

"I just want to take some pictures of them," she stated.

Samantha bristled. She immediately lost her charming "can I help you" smile. "I'm sorry, we don't allow photos. This is an art gallery and all of our merchandise is original, made by local artists."

She pointed to the discreet sign on the wall: "NO PHOTOS, PLEASE"

The woman was indignant. "Well, how am I supposed to get an idea of how I can make one of these, if I want to make a copy?"

"You sign up for a rat class. I will gladly take your name and get you on the list." She tried to get friendly again. "The Yarn Shop will be having their next class begin in January. What's your name?"

"I don't want to make a rat. I just need to photograph them. I work for a company in China that copies current ideas and trends. Your rat people should be complimented and thrilled that somebody has an interest in what they made! I have duplicated everything from handbags to hair ribbons, and all kinds of toys!"

Samantha's mouth shot wide open. "You mean, you want to copy the rats? A copy cat? A counterfeiter? Here in my Art Gallery in Gandville?"

"What's so hard to understand? Look at these boots!" She held one leg up to show off her footwear: "These aren't really UGGS; they just look like it. Thanks to my company and my ingenious friends; not to mention my hard work, everyone can actually afford a pair! Instead of paying $200, you can buy them at Walmart for $29.95! Where's the crime in that? This is America, lady!"

Samantha was floored. Her mouth remained open but no sound came out. She was speechless. A rip-off artist right here in her shop!

She was also scared to death Judy and DD would walk in the door any minute and discover this woman straight from the town of Evil City and want to shoot her on the spot.

Gathering her thoughts, she looked at the woman right in her eyes, squinted her own down to narrow slits, and simply stated with her lips very tight, "You can purchase a rat. You can not photograph a rat."

Evil looked up at the tree, then slowly back to Samantha. "How much?"

"Two hundred dollars per rat." She knew first, the woman would never pay that, and second, if she did, Judy could easily make another really fast and be two hundred dollars richer.

"Your crazy!" Evil screamed.

"And you're a knock-off artist just trying to make a fast buck in my store!" Samantha screamed back.

With that, the woman reached into the tree, grabbed Chloe by the neck, ripped her from the branches nearly snagging the string of lights along the way. She slammed her down on the cash wrap counter and tossed her VISA card on top of the rat. The credit card covered Chloe's face.

"Ring it up!" she shouted.

Samantha was shaking. "Oh my God," she thought. What was she doing? Mechanically, She went through the procedure telling herself: "Stay calm. Breathe, breathe," Then scan the card, and then, oh, she nearly forgot. She took another deep breath and looked up. "I need an ID," she asked in a much more quiet controlled tone. Samantha was calm now. Better. Breathing helps.

The woman impatiently stood on one foot, switched to the other foot, sighed heavily, then reached in her fake Calvin Klein wallet and pulled out her Texas driver's license, handing it over to Samantha for inspection.

"Margaret Spencer, 533 Beacon Avenue" Samantha took it all in. Fancy address; right on the waters edge. Everyone knew Lake Grandville was actually the Grand River, created by the Grandville dam a few miles to the South.

The town was architecturally nestled along the river's path, and the most prestigious homes had "deep water frontage" on Beacon Drive so they could dock their yachts.

Grandville was one of many of the famous Texas man-made lakes. Like a hidden jewel, this one was truly beautiful with the surrounding cliffs and tall pine trees. The name fit: It was truly a grand river, and a grand town.

Cool as a clam, Samantha stored all of this in her head for future reference.

Breathe, Samantha, Breathe. Purposely taking time and even smiling again now, without a shake of her hand, she slowly wrapped Chloe in gold-trimmed tissue and placed her in a special embossed pink Art Gallery gift bag and tied the handles with a soft satin ribbon.

She looked at the soft little rat in her crocheted dress peeking from the bottom of the bag. Samantha wanted to give her a final kiss goodbye, but she couldn't in front of Evil standing there right in front of her.

In a flash, the woman grabbed the bag from Samantha's hands, looked up at her surprised expression, gave her a last minute sneer, and was out the door. All that was heard was the soft chime of the doorbell as the gallery door clicked closed and Chloe was gone forever.

Samantha stood riveted in place with her arms still out and looked at the ceiling.

"Oh my God." Was all she could think or say.

Evil passed Judy and DD walking up to the art gallery door on the sidewalk. They smiled at her; she didn't give them the time of day.

They opened the door and entered all smiles with a burst of joy and the door chime ringing happily.

"Hey, hey, hey! We've got tacos! We've got salsa and chips! Do you have wine for us to celebrate?"

Chapter Twelve

Tragedy Strikes

Samantha stood in the middle of the gallery store with a blank stare.

Her mouth was open, her complexion was ashen and she didn't say a word as her friends entered the gallery.

Immediately, Judy and DD knew something was wrong. "What's wrong? What's happened? Are you okay?" asking simultaneously.

"Yes. Er, no." Hesitation. Samantha looked at her friends and tilted her head. "Did you see that lady leaving the gallery just now?"

Judy shook her head. "Not really; we were talking and carrying the tacos and salsa." She put the party food down on the counter and walked closer to Samantha. Clearly, something was wrong.

"What happened?"

The three ladies stood in the middle of the store. Thankfully, there were no other customers.

"Did she steal something?" DD wondered and scanned the merchandise.

"Well, kind of. She paid for it, but she still stole it."

Both together, "What?"

"Chloe."

"Chloe?"

"Yes, yes, Chloe! She bought Chloe!"

"Oh my God. How? Why? How much did she pay? Where did she go? She really bought Chloe? But Chloe wasn't for sale!"

Now, all three were talking at once and asking the same questions almost shouting at each other. They both nearly levitated off the floor.

Shaking, Samantha said, "Let's sit down. Go put the CLOSED sign in the window. I need to tell you the whole story."

They did just that. Quietly, Judy shut the gallery door, and put the sign in the window. DD got two chairs and they all went to the back room and joined Samantha at her desk.

Sir Reginald stared down at them from his perch on the printer; his usual spot next to the computer. Samantha explained the nightmare's details, right to the very end when Evil grabbed the bag from her hands and stormed out of the gallery. Samantha looked up at them. "Chloe is really gone," she said finally.

Everyone was in shock. Judy was speechless and let out a breath. DD spoke first. "Wow. The good news is, Judy made $200 today. The bad news is, Chloe was her very first rat and she will be hard to replace without a lot of trauma."

Tears started in the corners of Judy's eyes, then trickled down her cheeks. She wiped them away with the back of her hand. "Do you think if I called her to explain, she would return Chloe? I could make her another one."

Samantha looked at Judy tenderly and shook her head back and forth.

"Not this lady. It does't matter WHAT rat she has, Chloe the original or a replacement Chloe. Remember, she is going to copy Chloe for a company in China that will make thousands of Chloes and probably sell them for $5.99 at Walmart!"

She kept apologizing. "I didn't know what to do, and I NEVER thought she would actually BUY Chloe for $200! I am SO SORRY! SO, SO SORRY!"

Both gave her a supportive hug. The three just held each other for a moment. "You did the right thing. Nobody could have guessed something like this would happen, and I may have done the very same as you," comforted Judy.

DD jumped in and agreed. "I think you did great, actually.

You thought on your feet! Judy has two hundred dollars instead of nothing, with that woman storming in here, taking a photograph and running out!"

All three were shaken and heartbroken; certainly not in the mood now to party. They each needed time to think about what had happened, and how they would deal with the loss. "Let's get back together tomorrow" they agreed.

Slowly and mechanically, they put the tacos and salsa in the fridge; the chips on the shelf. They would all have wine at home by themselves that night. A lot of wine. And they would think about what had just happened.

Samantha pulled the plug on the tree lights, and Judy and DD picked up their tote bags, gave each other a last hug, shut the gallery door with the CLOSED sign now swinging in the window, turned off the last lights, and left. The doorbell barely made a sound.

Tic, tic tic. The corner clock worked its magic. Outside, the Courthouse tower clock struck the midnight hour. Darkness. Sadness loomed from every corner; the air was thick with it: you could almost touch and feel it. When the lights popped automatically on it was still darker than ever before. There was just such a feeling. The rats knew it. Something was wrong.

They wiggled their feet and stretched their arms high and out to their sides. One by one, they turned their heads around looking up and down taking in their new location in the Christmas tree. What a tangled mess they were in!

"Where THE HELL ARE we?" Sheriff TEX was first to shout something out this time. He was struggling somewhere in the middle of the branches. He was tangled up and wrapped with an electrical cord, and a light was wrapped around his boot.

Then, the same question was asked by three or four rats, all at the same time, and from all over the tree. "Where are we?" They were all very confused. Nobody knew where they had been relocated, nor for what reason.

The three Ratskateers bounded down from their place in the tree to the floor and looked up at the rest of the pack.

El Ratoncito and LeBeau stood next to Pierre, and Lenny pointed to the top of the tree. There was Amelia, sitting in her airplane on the highest branch, looking very confident in her pilot seat as the others seem to be scattered throughout the middle. Echo and Rattina hobbled over to each other; held each others hands while clinging to a branch.

They looked down on Sheriff TEX who had just untangled himself and jumped out onto the floor, nearly hitting the spinning wheel below.

"Ah repeat, WHERE THE HELL ARE WE????" Now Sheriff TEX was shouting very loudly. This woke up Sir Reginald in the back room. He hopped off the printer and came running.

Of course, he knew the situation; he had seen the tree last year and figured it out. "You all have become Christmas ornaments, in Samantha's annual Christmas tree, obviously!"

Sir Reginald stood there with TEX and the other three boys. They all searched the tree for their comrades and found Amelia easily; she was the tree top ornament, and there were Echo and Rattina just below her. Lenny was climbing toward them now, but where were Belle, Violet and Chloe?

They called their names. Belle was caught on a lace pillow ornament, over on the side of the tree. "Help!" She cried. Violet sat shivering right next to her.

Pierre ran up the tree with LeBeau and together, they freed Belle from her tangled pillow mess. "Oh, thank you, thank you! Merci, Pierre!", rat eyes batting. They held Violet gently and eased her down.

103

Echo and Rattina made it to the floor on their own, and they all huddled together at the bottom with Sir Reginald, who started to explain to Amelia how she should leave her airplane and exit the tree.

Sheriff TEX interrupted, "NOW, HOLD ON THARE!" He took three steps forward and started waving his hands over his head. "Ah got an idea! Ah got an idea! We could swing a rope up thare and lassoo the darn thing an haul it down!"

SirReginald ran to TEX. "No, no, no! It would only bring down more ornaments and the tree might even fall down! Don't do that!"

"Well, how's she gonna git down then, ya little smart a...."? He stopped because ladies were present. TEX cooled his boots. He may be a Texan, but he was a gentlemen Texan.

From the top of the tree, came a soft voice from Amelia. "Everyone, just calm down! You have all forgotten! I told you I knew how to fly this thing!" And with that, a soft hum was heard from above, and the Lockheed Model 10 Electra began to shake and move.

Amelia gunned the little engine and it rolled forward on a branch. The plane's weight bent the branch dangerously low, then about the time it was about to fall off the branch altogether, it caught the air current from the overhead ceiling fan and lifted right off the Christmas tree. Amelia Earrat was flying through the art gallery and buzzing her fellow rat friends below! Grinning ear to ear, she waved her arm below, "Bonjour mes amiees!"

All the rats were screaming below and waving their hands. "Amelia, land! Land!" She was having a ball, and they were all scared to death.

Sheriff TEX shouted, "Yeee- hah! You go, gal!" He was
jumping up and down and laughing himself silly.

She circled the gallery twice. "Woo-hoo!" Finally, Amelia
brought the plane to a stop right in front of the stairway
and hopped off. "Told you!" She said with confidence
hopping from the plane, walking up to them.

What was that white thing around her neck; a scarf? The
rest of the rats all came running and gathered around her.
"Thank goodness you are all right!"

They all congratulated Amelia and checked each other
over. They were all okay, even though a little shaken.
Everyone was accounted for except Chloe.

Pierre was first to ask. "Ou est mon Cherie Chloe?" He
called, "Chloe? Chloe? Mon Cherie? Ma petite Cherie? "

Nothing. Silence. No response; no Chloe. No Pierre's
missing love. Then everyone called againtogether; loudly:
"CHLOE-EEEEE-EEEE?" Nothing.

They ran through the shop. They ran up the tree. LeBeau
and Ratoncito climbed the yarn rope to the loft and
searched there. Everywhere they went, they called and
called. No Chloe. No Chloe the rat anywhere. Chloe was
missing. Chloe was gone.

"She wouldn't have run away," said Sheriff TEX.
"Everyone knew she loved Pierre; that was obvious."
He looked over at Pierre, rolling his eyes."

Pierre just stood there, his eyes misting up. Softy, he asked
everyone, "Ou est ma petite Cherie?" He looked up at the
ceiling; he could hardly speak, "Chloe, C'est moi!

Regardez! C'est Pierre! It's Me! Look! It's Pierre! I love you!"

Sir Reginald was on his feet, spinning in a circle, his brain on full speed ahead.

"THINK, THINK!" he told himself.

"If she's not here, and she's not hiding, maybe she was sold?" he thought. He ran to the cash register, opened the drawer and checked the cash. Nothing here; looks like it was a slow day. Then he looked at the day's credit card receipts.

There it was. A VISA transaction for one rat: $200 ($200?!) Sold to a Margaret Spencer at about 4:00 PM yesterday. Holy cow! Holy bloody cow! Chloe has been sold! And now he had to tell his friends, and especially, Pierre. His love was really gone.

Chapter Thirteen

A Long night with a plan

The rats just collapsed where they stood. One of their comrades was taken from them, and they had no control. They all wondered the same thing: "Who would be next?"

Sir Reginald recognized Pierre was in no shape to remain French teacher for the day; and Sheriff TEX meant well, but his limited intelligence level would not get them all very far. He knew they had to act fast. Who knew what would happen to Chloe if they didn't rescue her soon? Reginald shuddered at the thought.

Gathering everyone's attention, "WE HAVE TO DEVELOP A PLAN!" he announced, and hopped up on a display counter. Very sure of himself he continued, "First, we must all stick together, and find a way to locate Chloe and get her back. The question is, HOW."

Pierre was beside himself with grief, and couldn't even speak. He turn around and sat on the floor behind most of the group in desperation. He noticed the chef's hat on LeBeau. "Quelle chapeau!" What a hat! Was all he said.

LeBeau heard Pierre's comment and knew the French word for hat. He touched the top of his head and grabbed at his head. "What the heck? Whose idea was this?" He tossed the hat across the floor and it landed in front of the tree. His spoon had already fallen to the floor when he escaped the branches and now the hat rested gently against the spoon.

Everyone focused and now listened to Sir Reginald's every word. Very convincing, his English accent seemed to confirm his intelligence, and what they all needed to do.

He spun into high gear. Quickly, he scampered back to the computer and looked up the VISA transaction. By clicking on the name, and imputing the drivers license number, he was able to access all the data about Chloe's purchaser: her name, where she lived, even her telephone number! Sir Reginald was a genius! "Ah, technology!" he said.

"Now, let's put our heads together and think. We need to get to Margaret Spencer's house at 533 Beacon Avenue. How are we going to do that? Any ideas?"

The rats all looked at each other with blank stares.

Then Lenny had a thought: "We need transportation that operates at night," he said. He was right. The rats only lived from midnight to six in the morning. Grandville was a sleepy little town with little or no night life. "Who operates at night? What businesses are active that we could get some help from?" he asked.

"Bakeries!" shouted Echo. "Bakeries make bread and deliver to stores in the morning! We could hop on a bakery truck!"

"Yes, but how would the truck get to Margaret Spencer's house?" asked Rattina. "We need help from some kind of delivery service," She said.

"Now, we are on to something!" Sir Reginald was spinning around in a circle again. He was pacing. He was thinking.

His rat brain worked at warp speed. He suddenly stopped and looked up.

"I've got it!" shouting to everyone, "FED-EX!...... FED EX!"

"Fed-Ex?" they all asked together.

"Yes! Federal Express!" You know! It's the delivery service ALL businesses use to ship their goods overnight! "We have to send ourselves by Federal Express overnight to Margaret Spencer's house! It's GENIUS!"

The rats were totally confused. Sir Reginald had to explain the process. "Samantha, Judy and DD send and receive merchandise EVERY DAY here at the store."

He ran back to the office and returned with an armful of pink paper receipts that tracked the Yarn Shop and Art Gallery shipping orders to customers all over Texas, and some as far as Japan. He leaned forward with confidence and explained, "We will send ourselves in a FED-EX BOX to Margaret Spencer!"

"Ah, come on!" shouted Sheriff TEX. "Yer nuts, Reginald! Rats in a BOX!? That's BULLSHIT!"

Others expressed their doubts, too. The general concession was "It won't work."

Echo was scared to death, and so were Belle and Rattina, who said they were claustrophobic. (And where did this come from?)

Amelia, on the other hand, thought the idea was brilliant and couldn't wait to get started. She walked closer to Sir

Reginald. "What kind of package will we be?" She was curious.

Reginald was talking very fast, now. "Federal Express has their own boxes and labels. Samantha keeps a stack of them in the back room where I live. She packs stuff in them every day, addresses the labels and the Fed-Ex guy comes about ten in the morning and picks it up. They have a regular account with them! We just have to jump in a box, and we will be picked up, and on our way!"

Sir Reginald was so sure of the plan, he seemed to have every answer. Except one. If they were all in the box, who would seal it shut and address the label? And how would they get the box on the counter? And, wouldn't they get hurt bouncing around inside the box?

Back to the drawing table. Everyone thought. Now they were a team. You could hear their little rat brains ticking away. Silence. They were all thinking, now. Sir Reginald was clicking his fingers on the counter top; tap, tap, tap: a sure sign that an answer was forthcoming.

Slowly, he lifted his head up, and turned sideways, first checking on Pierre who was slumped on his side in his deep depression, doubtful anything would save his love.

Sir Reginald leaned forward. Everyone listened intently. "Here's what we do: We put the box in place on the counter to be picked up and get all settled inside; but before that, we will have addressed the label first, and leave it next to the box that we have already jumped in! Tomorrow morning, Samantha will see the label, and think she must have forgotten to put it on the box (she does this all the time), then, she sticks it on, and whoosh! Off we go! "In his best English accent, he shouted, "ITS TRULY BRILLIANT!"

Everyone looked at each other. It just might work.

"Let's do it!" shouted Tex. Putting his hands on his hips, he rounded everybody up. "Let's go find us a box! We're gonna do it!"

With that, all the rats followed Sir Reginald to the back room, where he showed everybody the stack of boxes in the corner. "The labels are sitting here, right next to them. The Art Gallery account is already on line in the computer, so all I have to do is type the destination address in, put the label in the printer, and voila! (He was speaking a little French by now) We are addressed to go!" And then he hopped on the computer and went to work.

TEX handed Sir Reginald a label. "Let's get er done!"

Collectively, the rats pulled a box down from the corner, and pushed and shoved it through the store maneuvering it around the display racks and stands until reaching the front service counter. Now the trick was to get it up on top and next to the cash register where Samantha would see it to be picked up.

El Ratoncito was now the hero. His experience with previous climbing and sneaking around with his nighttime children's tooth job was paying off. He bit a tiny hole in one corner of the box flap; hardly enough to see, but big enough to slide a string of yarn through it so the box could be hoisted up to the counter's edge.

"Okay, go find me a strong skein of yarn for a rope!" He directed.

Sir Reginald came out waving the finished label in his arms. "I see we are making progress!" He said. "We can use my yarn rope in the corner to run up to the loft and get the same hemp skein we made before; we know it will hold all of us!"

The Ratskateers, now elite marathon rat runners, took off at the same time for Reginald's rope, but TEX stopped them. "Y'all, we need just one of you to go up thare, not a whole wagon load!"

Ratoncito took the lead, and up he went; grabbed the hemp skein and tossed it over the loft edge. Waiting with their arms stretched upward, LeBeau and Lenny caught it before it hit the floor, and were off to the service counter reaching the box just as Ratoncito made it back to the group. He took the end of the yarn and thread it through his bitten hole. Pulling the yarn through, he came up with just enough length to create a winch and hoist system.

Then Lenny and LeBeau climbed to the top of the counter with one end of the yarn, and started pulling. "WE NEED MORE WEIGHT UP HERE!" They shouted below. They were in hyper mode, alright.

Quickly, Everybody responded and headed for the counter top. Even Pierre gathered enough strength to become a partner in the rescue team. They worked together as one. It was "Team Rat" all the way. They should have had T-shirts!

SirReginald scanned over the counter top to the team below. "HEAVE!" He shouted. "ONE, TWO, THREE, HEAVE!"

Pierre was now suddenly alive with newfound strength. He gritted his little rat teeth, and flexed. He jumped up and down, "UN, DEUX, TROIS, TIREZ!"

In little short jerks, the box began to move upward. Slowly, slowly, and with each command from Sir Reginald in English and Pierre in French, the box reached its destination on top the service desk.

The rats dropped the yarn line. Mission accomplished. They all collapsed in a heap. "WHEW! WE DID IT" Pierre looked at his comrades with a knowing look. Oh, he was back to himself, all right.

"Certainement!" he said with complete confidence. But of course.

"Now what?" asked Rattina, and she looked at Sir Reginald.

"We get inside. All of us. And then, we get some tissue paper, smooch it all around us for safety and comfort, lift the skein of hemp on top of us to hide under, add some more tissue for added padding, and then, the last thing we do, is place the label on one of the box flaps to look like it needs to be sealed better. Then, we wait for Samantha to finish the job. "

It sounded easy enough. The girls jumped down and returned with sheets of pink tissue.

TEX complained, "Ah don't lack pink! It's not very sheriff-y"

"Too bad," they said. "It's the Art Gallery trademark tissue, Sheriff!"
"Well, then, gist don't put a bow on me!"

More tissue was needed. The girls scurried back and forth, bringing two or three sheets at a time with each trip, and

113

they all took turns getting into the box and packing the tissue around them tightly so they wouldn't get hurt. Their little rat hearts were pounding and they were breathless.

The hours sped by quickly. Finally, they all made it inside, and Reginald was the last to secure the hemp, stuff extra tissue on top, and make sure the label was ready for Samantha.

They made it. They were now addressed to go. All they needed was a few hours of rest inside the box, and for Samantha to arrive on time and secure that label. They would then be on their way to rescue Chloe and see Pierre smile again.

It was dark inside the box. The rats peaked at each other, and whispered, "Are you all right, Pierre?" They asked.

"Oui, merci beaucoup. Je suis fatigue." He was grateful, and of course, exhausted.

Only an hour to go, then, Tic, tic, tic. Outside, the Courthouse clock performed right on schedule, then peace and quiet again in the Art Gallery.

Chapter Fourteen

Fed Express Overnight Delivery

Samantha tried everything to get in a better mood. On her way to the store she bought a Grande instead of her regular Tall coffee at Starbucks, and even splurged with a zucchini muffin, hoping the sugar boost would elevate her spirits, but she still was afflicted with the wounds of yesterday's Chloe disaster.

Talk about a bummer. She knew Judy was really being polite about the sale, but deep down she knew her friend was really upset about the loss. Who wouldn't be? There was nothing Samantha could do to make it better. She signed and convinced herself, "Time will be the best healer".

Geeze, it was already ten o'clock, and the first customer was following her in the door as she opened for business. A good sign for the day.

"Hi Samantha! Will Judy be here today?" It was Marna, LeBeau's Maker.

"Yep, today is one of her class days, so I am sure she will be here soon."

"Well, I'll just admire your Christmas tree while I wait." Marna walked over to the new addition to inspect. "Well, It's really nice!" she commented.

Not looking at the tree, Samantha stood at the cash register, turning it on for the day and getting her service counter all organized. "Well, just nice? what do you think about the rats?"

"What rats?"

"The rats! YOUR RATS! They are the ornaments!"

"I don't see any..."

Just then, the gallery door swung open and the bell on the doorknob chimed. It was Henry, the Fed Ex guy, and he was moving lightning-fast, as usual. Ignoring the store's interior, he quickly glanced at the service counter behind the cash register.

"Looks like you've got one for me" he said, pointing at the box with his electronic clipboard.

"Oh! I didn't see that there. Must be Judy's shipment." Samantha picked up the box, and only glancing up at Henry, handed it over without even looking at it.

"Well, Judy nearly missed getting the label attached. She must have been in a hurry." Henry gave the sticky label an extra push on top of the box and secured it. "That ought to do it!" Then, tucking the box under one arm, made the pick up notification in his electronic clipboard, and was back out the door in a flash.

Marna walked back up to Samantha. "Hey, I didn't see any rats," she said.

They both went back to the tree. Samantha looked closely; up and down; walked behind, looked up at the top for Amelia Earrat. No Amelia, no plane, and no rats. Not anywhere on her tree! "Where were they?" She wondered.

Samantha immediately thought Judy and DD were upset from the Chloe disaster and had come in and removed them. She didn't not want Marna or any other customer to know what had happened, so she didn't say another word. She would have a private discussion with her rat-knitter friends later.

Samantha turned to Marna, "Well, I thought Judy and DD were going to put them in the tree, but they must have changed their minds. It was a cute thought, anyway." She strolled away from the tree dismissing the conversation altogether. "They should be in soon."

Samantha's art and Marna's rats were two separate worlds under one roof.

Marna didn't have much interest in looking at the art; she has seen it a hundred times, so she headed for the stairway. Thank goodness she had the loft to lose herself in for a while, she thought. The loft was her personal sanctuary. Little did she know, it was everyones personal sanctuary! She had had a rough morning with her husband's family and wanted some time to herself, so she climbed slowly to her own little yarn heaven above to wait for Judy and her knitter comrades in crime.

Neither thought any more of the rats until Judy walked in.

"Marna's upstairs waiting for you." Samantha was a little short with her words. "When gathering session is over today, let's talk about the rats," she concluded. Judy looked at the tree, noticed the rats were gone, and thought, "Uh-oh, she must have changed her mind about the ornaments and needs to explain." Up she went, as Marna was already waving down at her.

117

Samantha busied herself with the Art Gallery duties, and Judy was already discussing Marna's knitting project.

The day got busier for both shop keepers, and thank goodness, sales were brisk all day. Things were definitely picking up speed for "holiday mode."

Before long, it was nearly closing time. DD had come in about four, and when the knitting duo finally had time alone, they discussed the rats disappearance in whispers in the loft.

DD leaned over and looked at Judy, "Where are the rats?"

"Shhh! I think she felt so bad about Chloe, she took them all down!"

"Where did she put them?"

"Don't know. Haven't had time to talk to her yet."

Samantha's last customer left with a big package and a smile on her face.

"That's what I call one stop shopping!" She laughed as she closed the shop door behind her.

Upstairs, Judy and DD heard her leave, and nearly bounded down the stairs with curiosity. "OK, how come you moved the rats?" They asked.

"I DIDN'T move them; I thought YOU did!"

"WE didn't!"

"YOU didn't?"

"NO!"

All three together, "Then who did?"

They looked at each other, and then around the room, as if they would pop out from some shelf on their own, and then they were all very quiet.

"What do you think?" Asked Judy. Samantha turned her head back and forth. "I have no idea. No one was here to buy them, and who would want to take them?"

"That woman who bought Chloe, that's who! Maybe she wants to copy ALL the rats!"

"Well, I've got her phone number from the sale. I can call her and ask her if she knows anything," Samantha suggested.

"Oh, I wouldn't do that." Judy thought that might be too accusatory. "That could get us in trouble; its like opening a can of worms."

They headed for the back room to sit down and discuss a plan. The back storage room-office seemed to be the place for assembling plans lately. If Margaret Spencer somehow got back in the store and took the rats, that would be robbery, and they didn't think she would take that risk. Besides, who knew if other things were missing from the gallery? Samantha hadn't had much time to do a complete inventory; she had just taken an "eyeball survey" of the displays and didn't notice anything out of order or missing.

They concluded with two things: First, they had to tell the rat makers; they had to know about Chloe and the remaining missing rats. Second, they needed to call the police. Out of respect, they decided, call the Makers first. Judy and DD split the list in half and sat down to make phone calls. Since Samantha owned the art gallery; she would call the police.

The Maker's reactions were all identical: first shock, then concern for Judy who had first lost Chloe in such a tragic way and then disbelief that someone would steal their treasured little rats. Why?! "Were they really all GONE?" They all asked the same question, over and over, except Geraldine, who just cursed in French. "Mon Dieu!" My God! But of course.

Judy finished her last call then looked at Samantha. "Time to call the Grandville Police Department."

In no time at all, a squad car pulled quietly up to the curb, and two officers climbed out, entered the shop and introduced themselves to Samantha. "Officer Dean and Officer Harris, Mam," they said together. Officer Dean tipped his hat very official-like, touching his badge at the same time. "We understand you have a problem." No sirens, no loud noise, no disturbance to anyone outside. Just their low voices in quick monotones.

Samantha looked at Judy and DD with a look that asked, "Are these guys for real?" There they were: Caught in a time flash. Suddenly it was 1967, and the scene turned to black and white. Sergeant Joe Friday and his squirrel-like partner Bill Gannon from Dragnet were standing right there like stick men in front of her.

Looking at her knitter friends and not the TV duo, she slowly walked to the front and quietly closed the door hanging the CLOSED sign in the window in one swift movement. They outlined in short form the story about the missing rats. At first, the officers listened intently about the possible robbery, then as the details unfolded, snickered about the merchandise in question and made ready to pack up and leave.

"You mean, you've called us about somebody stealing some little rat toys?" They looked at each other eyes rolling; it was obvious they had better things to do.

Judy and DD were indignant, standing very straight with their hands animating their dismay. "No! You don't understand!" Judy pointed her finger to Officer Dean. "Now look! These aren't some little ten dollar play toys! They are works of art; just like everything else in this shop! Take a good look! They are originals! People would pay a lot of money for them!"

"OK, okay...settle down, ladies. We get it." "We will see what we can do." Officer Harris slowly pulled out his note pad, rolled his eyes again, and reluctantly started taking notes and detailed descriptions of each rat. Monotone voice again, "The first rat, is 'FRENCH;' you say?"

Then, looking over his glasses at his partner Officer Dean, he began to write quickly, "Uh-huh, Uh-huh. One had a chef's hat and carries a spoon. The French one has a mustache and wears a French beret. Black you say. Name's Pierre." He looked up at the ladies and looked down again at his clipboard. Don't laugh, don't laugh. Scribble, scribble.

You could tell he wasn't getting every word down; he was just making the show. His moves were calm, sincere, and very professional; "just give these ding bats what they need," he thought, and continued with the descriptions of the girl rats. "One is a southern belle, and one is kinda like Mother Nature?" The ladies named each missing rat and detailed their descriptions.

"Excuse me." Officer Dean had to leave the shop "to get something" from the squad car; but really he had to escape and let the laughter explode from his body before he might burst right there in front of everybody.

"Oh, this one's a beauty!" he radioed back to the Chief, who joined in with the joke of the day. "Wait till the Grandville Daily Reader hears about this one!" The newspaper monitors all the police calls, they knew, and their office would be having a field day laughing, too.

Inside, Office Harris was rapping up. "We'll keep you posted, ladies, on any developments in The case, Meanwhile, if you hear or see of anything suspicious that might help us, let us know right away." He sounded convincing and very official. They both tipped their hats, made a u-turn, and left.

The scene returned to color and the present again.

"They think we are a joke!" screamed DD. "They think we are nuts!"

"We just love our little rats, that's all. They are like our little children."

"And now they are gone. ALL OF THEM. GONE."

All three women were speechless. They had no other words. They had no comfort to share other than the empty feeling they would carry in their hearts until they knew where their beloved rats were.

Chapter Fifteen

533 Beacon Drive

They all came running.

Even though the Makers were busy with last minute Christmas plans and projects that were on the critical "Gotta finish this today!" list, they dropped everything and made it a priority to gather at The Yarn Shop late Tuesday afternoon. Even though it was just about closing time, they wanted to hear ALL the details about their cherished missing rats.

"Well, What's the word?" Out of breath, Raspberry anxiously started the truck load of questions. She had semi-promised her little garden rat Echo to her granddaughter.

Now what would she do?

Mary Ellen's ranch boots made a distinctive stomp as she climbed the stairway, and she joined Marna halfway up. Together, they shouted upward to the group, "Any news?"

All the Makers were gathered about the table now, and all eyes and ears focused on their fearless leader. The troops had arrived and they all sat on the edge of their chairs.

Judy told them about her conversation with the Granville Dragnet Team, but there was really nothing more to report. The rats had simply just disappeared.

"All that was left were LeBeau's chefs hat and spoon, and Amelia's airplane!"

"Who would want all of our rats?"

"Why did they leave LeBeau's hat and spoon?"

"How did they get Amelia out of her airplane at the tree top?"

"And why did they leave her plane?"

Everyone was dumfounded; nobody had any answers. They just shook their heads and realized they couldn't do a darn thing about their rats. They decided the best thing to do was to go on with their other work projects for now and keep busy. Enjoy the holidays. Something would come up. Such a loss. They all felt so empty.

"One thing for sure, I don't want to make another rat! I want my Amelia back!" Said Anita.

"We've got to just dive into our projects and try to enjoy the holiday" suggested Sandy, and she picked up her half-finished sweater. "I've got to get this done before I take off in my RV and head down to Houston for a group rally."

They looked around the loft hoping their beloved rats were somehow misplaced, or hiding in a corner.

Geraldine glanced down at her Louis Vuitton tote resting at her feet. "I just miss Pierre so much! I never thought I would become so attached to this little guy!" She wasn't even speaking her flawed French.

They sighed. They hugged. The Makers knew they probably wouldn't see each other again until after

Christmas and they talked about their happy days of rat making.

"We had so much fun. How could anybody do such a rotten thing?" They wanted to know.

"They'll turn up," comforted Judy. "They've got to. We will just have to be patient and wait and see." She just didn't know what else to say; she knew they were heartbroken.

There was nothing more to say or do. It was time to pack up and head out. Samantha was making "closing up sounds" below.

The Makers gave each other hugs of hope, wished each other happy holidays sans their rats, and taking care with the stairway, slowly and silently made their way down and out the door. The doorbell chimed softly.

Outside, The clock tower in the Square rang it's familiar midnight song, and The Yarn Shop corner clock ticked right on cue simultaneously. All was dark and quiet in Grandville.

All quiet and dark except at 533 Beacon Drive. At this unsuspecting residence, a lot of action was about to take place, and things might not ever be the same at this address.

The ride in the Fed Ex truck was a rough one. The rats were more than rearranged; they were on top of each other, some were flat on their backs, and others were turned around and in each other's faces. But all was still now and the box had ceased to move anymore. But the contents did.

"Obviously, we didn't pack enough tissue around us!"
Belle and Echo's noses were touching each other, and they
stared at each other eyeball to eyeball.

Each rat gave themselves a little shake, wiggled their feet
and hands, turned their heads.

They were all okay.

Sir Reginald carefully untangled himself from Pierre,
whose beret had traveled over to LeBeau's shoulder and
wedged itself in the corner of the box.

"We are here! " He announced. "We can lift the top of the
box flap over Amelia's head and get out on this side." He
squeezed along the side, working his way past Lenny and
climbed on Pierre's shoulders. He lifted his arms up to
demonstrate.

"We all can push up from here."

Pierre grunted with the extra weight.

"Mon Dieu! Aidez moi, sil vous plait!" I need help!

The other rats wiggled over to Pierre and together they
huddled and pushed upward with their arms and legs until
the box flap burst open . Then Sir Reginald climbed higher
to peek out. It was so dark he couldn't see a thing.

"Where are we?" They all asked from below.

Echo was on the bottom of the heap and worried about
being trapped.

"If we all stand on each other, who will be left in the box?"

126

"Simple!" Answered Sir Reginald. He leaned over to the right side of the box. "We all get on this side of the box and our weight will turn us on our side, then we just simply walk out!"

They all began to move to the right. "It's working! It's working! Its like being on a boat and running to starboard!"

The box tipped over. It worked so well, they all just toddled out into the darkness in shock. They were here. They made it, and had arrived to save Chloe. They just had to find her, but where to begin?

The rats stood in a circle bending their heads and adjusting their eyes. Looking up, they could see the stars above them and knew they were outside on a front porch.

"Let's push the box away so it can't be seen" suggested Sir Reginald. The Ratskateers obeyed immediately. The group pushed the box to the side of the porch until it lodged itself on a lawn sprinkler and wouldn't move any further.

"That'll do it."

"Now what?" asked Ratoncito, holding his hands on his hips.

"How about we just start calling Chloe? Maybe she will hear us" responded Echo.

Belle and Amelia nodded and began together. "Chlooooooeeeee!"

"Nah, that won't work. She has to be somewhere inside this house; we've got to get inside."

"Let's go! We will find the way in soon enough" Sir
Reginald led the way from the porch around to the side of
the house. They looked up and down the wall looking for
an opening. Nothing.

The group scampered around the corner and were now at
the back of the house. There was a security light above
that suddenly turned on above their heads. Their
movement must have triggered it, and they could see a
small square entrance at the bottom near a back door.

"What's this?" Amelia was pushing the flap of some kind of
opening. She pushed a little harder and fell into the house.

"A doggie door!" hollered Sir Reginald. *"It's for pets to
come and go! Be careful! They must have a dog or a cat
here, or worse, both!"* He screamed.
⟨

Amelia lay on the floor flat-eagle on her stomach.
"Whew!" Where was she? She shook her head and crawled
to her feet. The floor was wood, and her crash alerted
someone near her with a lot of fur. A low growl came from
the fur. She backed up. *"Oh My God..."*

Flash was an old, border collie. He was a friendly guy;
just big, just old, Amelia told herself. Probably hard of
hearing. She slowly crept backwards to the doggie door
where her comrades waited outside and held their breath.

Ratoncito was closest to Amelia and reached his arm
through a crack in the door. He grabbed her airplane
scarf, still wrapped around her neck and pulled quickly.
Out popped Amelia and they all ran together around the
corner and hid along the side of the house.

Flash sauntered through the doggie door slowly, losing track of the rats. His sixteen years had caught up with him. He looked around; Flash, The Senior Citizen Dog, had even lost his scent. "Let's see, now....what was I looking for?"

"What next"? Out of breath, the rats were all panting and wondering the same thing. How were they to get inside, if Flash was guarding the door?

"Let's try it again, only we've got to distract him, somehow." They worked their way back along the side of the house to the door. Flash was still outside, and wondering about the patio looking for his newfound chase toys. They took this miraculous window of time, and together slipped silently through the doggie door that led inside to the dining room.

The rats adjusted their eyes again. There was a little night light plugged into the wall in the hallway. They moved forward.

"Chloeeeeee" They whispered.

"Shhhhhh!!!!!" Not so loud!" warned Sir Reginald.

"We must be very, very quiet!!"

They went down the hallway and began peeking in each doorway. A bathroom. A bedroom. Another bedroom. Someone was sleeping here and she turned her head. This disturbed Wayne, who had snuggled up at the foot of the bed with her. He lifted his head and squinted his big yellow eyes in question.

Wayne was lazy. He was the original Cheshire cat; wore a continuous "What do you want; please do not wake me up right now" look on his face.

She patted him with her foot, "Go to sleep, Wayne, and don't bug me."
Wayne laid back down and began to purr.

The rats tiptoed even lighter, now. This was scary. Beyond scary. They could be goners in a mouthful, just like that.

The next room was some kind of office. A work room, of sorts. Very messy; stuff was everywhere, stacked in piles around computers and printers. A couple of telephones, along with a big fax machine. Red and blue and little green lights blinked from each of the office equipment gadgets.

The rats had to work their way through the chaos of clutter, and at once they all recognized the Art Gallery pink bag sitting in the middle of the table.

"Chloe!" They all screamed aloud.

Wayne looked up. "What was that?" he jumped from the bed and padded into the hallway.

The rats did not move. Then they saw the bag wiggle and fall over sideways. Chloe peeked her head out and stared at her comrades. She mouth opened to shout something, but Sir Reginald held his finger to his mouth in warning, his eyes wide open with fear.

He mouthed his words, "DON'T MOVE!"

Chloe stopped in her tracks, and looked at the rescue team.
They were all there. A thousand questions ran through her
furry head all at once. "How, when, why...!" Then she
saw Pierre with his little rat hands crossed over his heart.

"Mon Cherie!" Pierre whispered, and held his arms out to
her. "Je suis voici!" "I am here!"

Wayne creeped closer and crouched in position to pounce.
He lifted his lips. Now you could even see his teeth.

Everyone held their breath. El Ratoncito Perez (he was
Catholic) crossed his heart to God to say goodbye to this
world. It would all be over soon.

Then, in lightening speed, LeBeau grabbed up a cell phone
laying on a stack of magazines and threw it down the
hallway. The phone hit the wood floor hard, then bounced,
hit the hallway wall, slid a couple of feet and landed in the
hallway bathroom. A tile floor. Oh great, lot's of noise
now.

Simultaneously, Wayne leaped up with LeBeau trailing
right behind Wayne's tail, and as Wayne jumped through
the bathroom door, LeBeau pushed the bathroom door as
hard as he could. For a human this would be a piece of
cake, but for a little rat it just barely closed and clicked, but
it was enough, and Wayne was trapped inside the
bathroom.

Turning on his toes, LeBeau sped back to his group in the
office.

My God, where did he learn to do this? He was THE RAT
ATHLETE!

They were all huddled together at the bottom of the table, and Chloe now looked down at them from the edge of the table above. The rats formed a circle, held their arms together forming a net. "Jump! Jump!" They shouted .

Chloe closed her eyes, held her breath pulled her arms in tight and leaped outwards and down. It was a perfect landing.

"Who needs a parachute? " Amelia asked.

There were hugs and tears of joy. Pierre held Chloe to his chest. Together again!

"We must leave right now!" Hollered Sir Reginald. He was waving his arms back and forth, jumping up and down. Wayne was starting to meow.

The cell phone's hard landing had effected the device as it was starting to buzz. The cat pawed the phone around on the bathroom tile floor, and the buzzing kept going. Wayne meowed harder and batted the phone against the bathtub. Bang!

Now Margaret was awake. Flash came bounding through the doggie door, and chaos was now in full swing. "What the hell....."

The rats ran down the hall just as Margaret came out of the bedroom, rubbing her eyes. Flash ran past them in a blur, half-blind and hard of hearing. He knew something was up with Wayne, but not sure about the buzzing sound.

Like a bolt of lightning, the rats shot down the hall, through the living room and dining room, past the table and chairs and dove through the doggie door in one big cloud of fur.

They made it. Scramble under the bushes. Can't be seen or heard.

Safe in the backyard, now they could at least take proper time for hugs and kisses.

Pierre grabbed Chloe and pulled her close. "Je t'eme, Chloe." "I love you." "Donnez votre bras; (give me your arms), and I will never let them go."

"Okay, y'all can do all that huggy stuff later!" Sheriff TEX had had enough of the gooey, and he asked Sir Reginald, "So what's next, boss?"

"We'll find a place to rest today," and he reminded everyone what time it might be. They didn't have much time left.

"Sound's good ta me, Ah think we are all purty tired." With that, Sheriff TEX sat right down on the ground, feet spread out straight in front of him on a stone pathway. He looked down through his boots and over the lighted path. The light beam led like an arrow straight to the water's edge.

"That way!" He pointed.

They looked up grabbed each others' hands and arms, and all started walking down the path, which led to a covered dock with the most beautiful yacht parked under the roof.

Chapter Sixteen

Margaret Spencer

"Well, crap!"

Margaret stomped her way down the hall, off balance and halfway bumping into the wall on either side, not fully awake yet. She asked questions to nobody there:

"What was that noise?" "Where's Wayne?" That damn cat.

"Now what is he up to!" She could hear him in the bathroom and he was probably chasing a mouse again.

"I'm gonna kill that damn cat!"

"Well, what's your story this time?" She opened the door and looked at Wayne, who now just sat there looking up to her, content to leave the cell phone behind the toilet where he had cornered it. Since it had stopped buzzing, Wayne was now bored and just wanted back in bed. He nuzzled up to Margaret and began rubbing her pajama leg back and forth with his body with a purr. She bent over and picked him up and petted behind his ear. "Let's go, Killer," she sighed and they padded back to bed.

The only time Margaret Spencer went out her front door was to pick up the Dallas Morning news and any other papers that got thrown her way. She retrieved her mail from her car and drove straight into the garage, closing the automatic door in one single movement as she parked the car.

She did not visit with neighbors; they asked her too many questions, like the meaningless "Oh Margaret, how ARE you doing?" Some waved to her, but she most often did not return the gesture. Sally Benson, her neighbor of ten years had always tooted her car horn when she went by, but she stopped doing this several months ago when Margaret stopped honking at her. It had been this way since her divorce two years ago.

She lived alone and liked it that way.

"BDWB" (Before divorce with Bill) they were quite the social couple. They looked like they belonged on a magazine cover of the well-traveled. There were parties, and clubs, and the neighborhood social get-togethers they hosted from their lavish home and waterfront paradise; complete with oversized flagstone patios with multiple umbrella tables, winding pathways, the shoreline dock lined with big trees and walkway lights, and of course, the boat. The big, beautiful boat. "It doesn't get any better than this."

It was still there, parked at the dock; a daily reminder of what once was: the extravagant lifestyle of a couple admired by everyone who visited. There was a successful bed and breakfast guest home on either side of her house that touched the Lake Grandville shores, like hers did. They were always full; no vacancies here. While visiting the B & B, guests would gaze across the hedges and lawns to Spencer's "life on the greener side." What a life they had. Oh, they had it all. Very, very chic.

In a flash it was over. Everyone's heard the story a million times: There was the younger, more attractive woman, who was a part of her husband's fashion business: a model who caught Bill's and every other man's eye, only Bill was the only sucker. He actually believed her story, and followed her around like a puppy. Oh, he was good at deception, all right. For months, she didn't ever suspect a thing, then the small town gossip started.

"Did you hear...." "Did you see..." In no time at all, it was all over town, and she had become the laughing stock. Margaret just wanted to shrink away.

Well, after twenty years of a faithful marriage and working herself to death to build a thriving international business, she would take good care of sweet Bill. And she did. Thank God there were no children. Each had devoted themselves religiously to the fashion trend copy business, and were exceptional at it.

Bill and Margaret Spencer were world-renown. For security purposes, they did all their own research shopping, took all their own photos, designed and manufactured all their own prototypes, and sold them to Min-Chu International in Hong Kong for duplication. It was a very tight little business. They did it all, and all from a unsuspecting, unassuming waterfront home in Grandville, Texas. Who would have thought?

Margaret ended up with everything except Bill. House, cars, boat and the business . They were all hers now.

But so was the work. And it was all work these days for her alone; sometimes 24-7, and the strain and stress were taking their toll. It was exhausting and Margaret was nearly wiped out. Days like this Sunday were rare, and she relished the short window of time she stole for herself today. Now, more often, she wondered, "Is it all worth it?" She sure had her doubts.

No one had taken the boat for a ride since the divorce. With the settlement, Margaret got the boat, but not the expertise in boating or the courage or even the desire to learn. So it just sat there, gathering curiosity from the neighbors, stringy cobwebs on its sides, and murky gook on its bottom. Lapping gently against the dock.

BDWB, the boat was the star of their show: carrying their wineglass-toting friends to summertime destinations along the winding Grand River-Lake Grandville waterway to places of fun and frolic. There was lots to see and do along the way, but mostly, they traveled to various restaurants and art shows.

Everyone knew "Spencer's Spirit," pointing it out as they would cruise by. Such style. "There goes the happiest people in Grandville," they would say. "The jet set!"

Margaret knew she should sell it; but the thought was so finalizing; as if the boat would be the last bit of Bill and happiness left in her life. She loved Spencer's Spirit; she decorated it herself with fake Polo details and signature fabrics. After the boat was gone there would be nothing left to smile about, ever. Her work these days didn't make her happy either, and she dreaded each trip to Hong Kong.

Two days had passed since she opened the front door. Margaret stopped shy of the doorway and placed her full coffee cup on the hallway table. She knew there were probably several newspapers for her to collect this Sunday, and reading her favorite sections would take most the day.

She wouldn't even get dressed: just stay in her robe all day, read the paper, and vege. No work, no phone calls, nothing. Just her and her cat Wayne, would curl up and read the papers alone.

Margaret opened the door and stepped outside. Winter's cold blast hit her in the face. She was right, there were the two papers, plus the latest issue of the Grandville Reader; the little local piece that told of soccer games won and garden parties had and art shows forthcoming. Mostly family stuff, which she was never really into.

Quickly, she tucked them all under her arm and turned back to the door, just barely noticing the edge of a box sticking out of the shrubbery. The sides were rippled and the printing was streaked with water from the sprinkler. Leaves covered half of it. "Must have been there a while, with the looks of it," she thought, and kicked it further into the bush so it was hidden altogether. "Let the gardener get it," dismissing the thought. The door closed with a quiet click and she bolted the door to the outside world.

Margaret tossed the papers on an ottoman next to her favorite chair, then padded over to retrieve her coffee. Wayne waited patiently for her, and Flash was nearby in his soft bed. Perfect. Everybody was in their places.

She first read the business sections of both the Dallas papers and the Style sections of course, checking the latest in every trend out there from fashion to kids toys. This was her business, after all: Make sure she didn't miss anything. There was the usual Neiman Marcus and Macy's stuff, and a few galas to see what the Who's-who were wearing, but nothing much stood out to her.

Finding the rats in that little store on the square had been a fluke, and she recognized a hot item when she saw one. She would start working on that little girl rat this afternoon. It would be a chore; she knew she would need to take it apart to make a pattern. It was already getting late.

Folding up the papers, Margaret decided she hadn't missed anything in the fashion trend world in the past two days. No need to read the Grandville rag, she thought. "It's worthless." She rolled the smaller newspaper up in a wad and tossed it near the fireplace with the other papers; good kindling for a winter fire.

Chapter Seventeen

Headlines

The Grandville Reader carried the weekly Sheriff's Report Column, based upon police reports. Nobody actually did any real reporting these days. There were two small house robberies, two car accidents, and then, the rat story:

STORE ON SQUARE REPORTS ROBBERY

The Yarn Shop, located upstairs in The Art Gallery reported a recent theft: Nine small furry toy rats were removed from the shop's Christmas tree, valued at about One thousand dollars. No other merchandise was taken.

According to store owners, each rat was hand made by local residents, has a different appearance, and apparently are all collector items.

Back at Yarn Shop, Judy read the paper with disgust. "Thats it? Just a couple little paragraphs? They think it's a joke!" she slammed the paper down on the counter. Samantha walked up front from the back room and picked up the paper. Disgusted too, she looked up at Judy. "Why don't you offer a reward?" She asked.

Judy didn't stop to think to about it, reaching for her iPad she immediately texted her message to the Grandville paper:

**REWARD OFFERED
FOR MISSING CHERISHED RATS.**

**$500 PAID FOR RETURN OF MISSING
TOY RAT COLLECTION TAKEN FROM THE ART
GALLERY CHRISTMAS TREE!**

**PLEASE RETURN, NO QUESTIONS ASKED.
CONTACT: JUDY PAXTON
THE YARN SHOP ON THE SQUARE.**

She finished the text, imputing her credit card information for payment, then clicked "Send."

Now she joined the Makers in their quest for the truth and the return of their treasured rats; and she waited for the phone to ring...

Chapter Eighteen

A New Home

Sunday slipped by fast enough. Playing around all afternoon doing not much, Margaret barely had time to heat up a can of chicken soup for her combined lunch and dinner; before she knew it was four in the afternoon. Damn. She had procrastinated long enough; time to get started on that stupid rat. She just hated doing this work anymore.

First, Margaret had to take hundreds of photos from every angle, which took hours. Photography was critical as once she cut the piece apart to make a pattern there was no backing up. And she dreaded the "cut and paste" process. This involved intricately snipping each seam of the rat stitch by stitch, then steaming the fabric out flat on muslin to make a pattern. Then using manicure scissors, clip every piece to make up a pattern "kit" that would be personally presented to Min-Chu International. The photos and pattern kit would be assembled, along with the eyes and all the separate parts and materials used to make up the rat, and these would be packaged for presentation. Another reason the photos were so important.

Bill had previously "presented," and they would always combine the business trip with a little bit of fun time in Asia, but that was all over now. There was no more fun time for Margaret; it was all just work. Just get there, do the job and get home. She had stalled away the day long enough. Reluctantly, she headed into the office to begin.

The bag was where she dropped it, but on its side. She reached inside and felt around. No rat. "What?" She thought. She ripped out the tissue paper and through it on the floor. No rat. Well, crap! She must have dropped it. Backtracking to her car, she looked along the floor, then checked inside the car. No rat. She looked along the floor in the garage. No rat. She went back inside and tore the office apart. Maybe it fell behind the desk. Behind the fax machine. No rat. No rat. NO RAT ANYWHERE. "WHERE IS THAT DAMN RAT?!"

Margaret scratched her head, thinking. "How could this be?" I had it in the bag; I came right home. "It couldn't just DISAPPEAR!" BUT THE RAT IS GONE. "NOW WHAT?!"

She couldn't go back to the store; they already hated her, and if they found it they surely wouldn't tell her. Buy another? No way. They wouldn't sell her one for a thousand dollars. Her goose was cooked. What was she going to say to China?

"Damn! Why didn't I take a photo!" Margaret was beside herself; she just didn't know what to do. She had spent the past two hours looking for the damn rat, and now her only solace was a glass of wine to kill the dismay. She poured her first glass of red and drank it down. Signature Red. The real stuff. Better pour another.

It was a very dark night, but the lights along the pathway and the dock interior roof lights overhead provided enough illumination to see about the boat. The water was very still; not even a ripple. You could see the reflection of the boat's port side along the water. "SPENCER'S SPRIRT' waved back and forth up upside down on the surface. Great name for a boat, but now with not much spirit. A fish swam by under the boat and sucked on the bottom making a

knocking sound. Other than that, no other sounds.
Nothing. Just stillness.

*They were now far enough way from the Square that only a
faint chime from the Tower clock was recognized; but it
was there: ever so lightly, the sounds of midnight made
their way to the rats ears.*

*They awakened slower than usual; their wild day yesterday
had tasked each one, and they wanted to sleep more, but
they were also very excited. They wanted to explore their
new home; at least it would be home for a while. Each one
knew in their heart there was no Federal Express back to
The Yarn Shop loft; they were out of boxes; they were out
of ideas. For Now.*

*Pierre was always first. He thought he had to be, because
he was the teacher. But now the new hero was the brilliant
Sir Reginald, who catapulted them from one life to another,
you might say, "Overnight!"*

*Pierre didn't care; he slept next to his love again, and held
her hand. He promised Chloe he would never leave her
side ever again. He wiggled his toes, then stretched his
legs. They were sore, but they worked. He turned his head,
opening his eyes very wide. He noticed something with a
blue light across the cabin of the boat. It blinked on and
off; on and off, and read, "12:01 AM" It was the cabin
alarm clock sitting on a built in side table. "Ou est nous?"
Where are we? He asked aloud.*

*Sir Reginald rolled over. "We are in our new home!" He
hopped around the floor. "Get up, everybody! Here we
are! Here we are!" The rats all wiggled and stretched.
They turned their heads from side to side; each checking
their working parts. They looked cautiously around the*

boat salon: No Wayne the cat; no Flash the dog. Just them, alone and safe and together tucked inside a cozy new nest.

They had done it. Mission accomplished. The plan to escape The Yarn Shop and rescue Chloe had worked, and now they were here inside a beautiful boat on the water in Lake Grandville.

Chloe stood up. "I don't know how to thank you all enough!" she shouted. "Merci! Merci! Merci Beaucoup!" She looked directly at Pierre, then bent down to straighten his beret. He smiled from ear to ear.

The rats wiggled and worked their way to the center of the cabin's room. The rug was royal blue and very soft with little anchors in it. A large compass was stitched in the carpet center, and the rats took positions with Sir Reginald standing on North.

Pierre and Chloe stood on the South point, and the rest of the rats found a spot all the way around. They held hands in a circle on the compass.

"I guess we will be little river rat sailors for a while" comforted Sir Reginald.

"You're the Captain!" confirmed LeBeau from his position on the Eastern point. He looked across the floor and picked up a cap from a large vitamin bottle and placed it on Sir Reginald's head.

Everyone put their hands to their head and saluted Captain Rat with his new cap. Reginald bowed and saluted back. "Welcome home, mates!"

Ce ne pas le fini......mes amies! (This is not the end my friends!)